Dreams in Atlantis

By
Jessica Hill

AOS Publishing, 2024
Copyright © 2024

Jessica Hill

ISBN: 978 1 990496 64 6

Cover Design: Chanelle Poupart

Visit AOS Publishing's website:
www.aospublishing.com

Thomas

The villagers overflowing from the tavern grumbled and shook the floorboards with their anxious feet. Thomas held his breath before diving between a stout pair of legs, his hands sticking in the mead that splashed from raised mugs as he crawled through the forest of bodies pressed against each other. When he was finally able to take another breath, the stench of so many people crowded together burned his nose; there were as many odors as there were feet and none of them were pleasant. Still, a tangible excitement charged the air with energy that pulled the boy forward until he could stand near a corner table at the front of the room. The wood was slick with chicken grease and spit, and it creaked when the magistrate climbed up to get a better view of his audience. Most fell silent to hear his speech. Others grew more restless, as if they had heard his words before and were anxious to get on with it.

"We cannot stand for this kind of assault on our livelihood!" His jowls quivered as he spoke, his fist thrust into the air. "We cannot afford to feed the beast while our children's stomachs remain empty! The monster steals our sheep and leaves their carcasses at our very doors. How long before it takes our sons and daughters? How long before the bones of the young become flour for it's bread?"

Shouts of agreement rang sharply next to Thomas' head in tempo with the blood pounding in his ears. He whooped along with the grown men and women all around him. He wasn't about to let some creature from the depths of hell cook him up for supper, least of all without a fight.

"I am calling all able bodied men to join me now," the magistrate continued, pulling a shiny sword, sharp as though newly made, to pierce the air above people's heads. "We will hunt the monster down where he sleeps if we must. His head will be nailed upon a stake, as a warning to keep others of his kind away!"

"I will fight the beast!"

"His blood will soak my axe!"

"I will fight!" Thomas shouted out along with the other men declaring their prowess. For the first time that evening, silence descended upon the tavern. Thomas puffed out his chest in the face of the villagers' stare. "I can help trap the monster," he stated bravely.

The thunderous laughter battered his pride.

The magistrate raised a hand to quiet the room. "'Tis a noble gesture, lad, but the creature would likely be glad to pick his teeth with a wee thing like you. Your time will come to show us your worth. When you're a man, you will get your chance to fight."

Thomas glowered at the man on the table. The magistrate moved on from his misdirected insult, taking more volunteers as though the boy hadn't spoken at all. Face burning, Thomas shoved his way back to the fresh air outside. The night was warm - summer was well underway in these parts - but it felt cool in comparison to the anger coursing through him. He kicked the dirt beneath his leather shoes. He swung his arms and kicked the ground until his toes hurt and a cloud of dust had risen to coat the hem of his short trousers.

"What did you think would happen?"

Thomas rounded on his brother with fists clenched to his side. He sniffed and hoped the older boy wouldn't notice the trails his frustrated tears had left on his dirty cheeks. He wasn't about to wipe his face and risk admitting they were there at all. "I could help. There's no better trapper than me in the whole kingdom!"

Jack laughed, stepping away from where he leaned against the mud walls of the tavern. He draped a long, thickly muscled arm around his younger brother's shoulders. Jack towered over Thomas, even though he was only a handful of years older. Thomas didn't think fifteen was so much better than nine. "Oh, little brother. You'd be nothing but a flea in his porridge. Let the men handle ol' Thunder."

Thomas shook the weight of his brother's arm from his shoulder. "I'll show them the strength of my honour. You'll see."

Thomas stormed off into the night, his temper rolling off him in waves. His hoe and hatchet were where he had left them earlier in the evening: next to the game trail his family used to drive their sheep to water. Twice now, the beast had ambushed them along the trail and made off with their spring lambs. Both attacks had come in the early light of dawn.

"This time I'll be ready," Thomas swore to himself. He set to work, breaking up the ground with his hoe and scooping the loose dirt away with the wide edge of his hatchet. When the hatchet proved too slow, his own hands clawed at the earth until they bled.

The hole had started as a dip in the earth the afternoon before, but by the light of a waning moon it soon became a deep gash, oozing shadows into the already dark night. Though his hands wept and his back ached, Thomas kept working until the dawn glowed red on the horizon, and his trap was ready for his quarry.

The ground shook as the monster approached. Thomas shrank back into the shadows, holding his hatchet at the ready.

The monster, taller than any house in the village, lumbered into view on the tail of a terrified ewe that had been separated from the herd. Greedy hands reached out, catching the ewe by her hind legs. Her scream briefly stunned the early morning bird song into silence. The giant snapped the animal's neck. With hardly a glance in either direction, he prepared to drape it over his neck to carry back to his lair. The giant's lack of fear or remorse drove the exhausted boy back to the brink of fury. Thomas leapt out from where he hid amongst the brush.

"Why not try a taste of me, sheep-breath!" he hollered.

At first, the giant seemed surprised by the child who straddled the path before him. Then he smiled a wicked grin and his eyes filled with hungry delight. With a roar that sent the birds fleeing from the trees, he charged forward. Thomas didn't dare glance down to where he had covered his trap with woven straw and broken branches. Though his hands slipped against the wooden handle, he held his hatchet above his head and let out a battle cry of his own.

The giant's right foot came down on the hidden trap first. Thomas had misjudged the size of his adversary. The giant fell hard on his knees, catching his rib cage on the edge of the pit. His breath left his body in a sudden whoosh, blowing Thomas onto his backside.

Thomas recovered before his enemy. Raising his hatchet above his head, he screamed like a wild creature of the woods. With every ounce of strength still lingering in his limbs, Thomas brought the minuscule wedge of iron down towards the giant's head. When the blade carved into the monster's forehead, the force of it jarred Thomas' arm. The giant bucked from the blow, pulling the handle from the boy's grip. Thinking fast, Thomas grabbed his hoe from where it had been discarded nearby and swung it with all his might towards the giant's exposed jugular. Warm, crimson rain showered him with victory.

Jack found his brother on his knees, steam rising from the congealed blood pooling around him. "Thomas?"

"I told you I'd show 'em."

Jack looked up from his prostrate brother to the hatchet wedged above the massive corpse's eye. Jack took the handle, slick with blood, and pulled. Heavily muscled arms, strengthened from years of working the land with their father, strained briefly against the sickening suction of the wound before the crescent blade came free.

"It's dead?!"

Jack and Thomas looked up together to see the magistrate and his mass of angry villagers standing just up the path. Thomas' chest swelled and he rose to his feet. A proud smile tugged the corners of his mouth, his chin tilting towards the sky. The magistrate approached them with wonder and awe in his eyes. "You killed the monster," he breathed.

The villagers began to whisper, and Thomas moved to present himself to the magistrate. This was it. He had proved his worth. Now he could call himself not only a man but a hero! His joy was short-lived. In a single moment, the world shifted. The magistrate looked right through the young boy, through the pride and the bone-deep exhaustion, and took the wrist of the older brother.

"You saved your brother," the magistrate whispered in awe. Jack offered his brother a look of sympathy, but though his mouth seemed to work at speaking he did not deny the praise.

Something inside of Thomas broke. His breath left his body. He allowed himself to sink back to his knees as he watched his sibling's hand, still grasping the tarnished hatchet, raised above their heads.

"All hail the hero of Chesterfield!" The magistrate called out, giving Jack's arm an extra shake. The villagers' excitement grew, their hoots and cries of praise echoing in Thomas' hollow chest. "All hail Jack the Giant Slayer!"

Chapter 1

I watched Mandar twirl smoke off his tongue. It was like watching a thick, pink snake dance, curving out of his mouth as it chased the tendrils of silver and grey. I let it mesmerize me, until the smoke formed three blue rings. The rings floated in the air, dancing to the same rhythm as my hips, until they reached a perfect position in front of his face. For a brief moment, they lined up with a small, childhood scar marring the smooth skin of his forehead. *Bullseye,* I smiled to myself. Mandar noticed the twitch of my lips and licked his own with anticipation.

I kept up the slow sway of my hips, losing myself for a moment in the familiarity of the dance, the hypnotic seduction of the music in my ears. My arms were raised above my head, hands mimicking the smoke coiling around the dim candelabra floating above my head. I let one hand run down the length of my arm, my flesh responding to the feathery touch of my fingers against my skin, to rest gently on the top of my head. The moment I was waiting for had almost arrived. Mandar's eyes had become half-hooded shadows, the pupils fully dilated from the *ghanja* herbs I had sprinkled in his pipe earlier in the evening. The herbs weren't always necessary, but Mandar was a shrewd client, already suspicious about our last encounter. Once I noticed his head begin to bob in time with the rhythm of my body, I knew it was time to act. Keeping my voice low and full of promises I never kept, I began to coax him into the Dream.

"Do you know why my master sent me?" I asked, increasing the tempo of my dance. The speakers in the walls created ripples in the air with every bass note. I took a sliding step forward, then another, until one bare knee brushed against my mark's leg.

Mandar groaned with anticipation. "Because I am the best damn lawyer in the city."

"You are, aren't you," I purred, leaning over to drag my silver-painted nails gently up the front of my legs. Mandar leaned forward to soak up the scent of the flesh between my breasts. "I'm going to show you exactly how good a lawyer you are. I'm going to show you how much my Master appreciates your efforts on behalf of the Collier family."

Mandar lapped it up, taking another drag on his pipe before setting it aside to play with other, more demanding things. I held his gaze, waiting for the window to open. When I saw it, the infinitesimal crack of light in his eyes where my soul could slip into his mind, into the Dream, I readied myself to pounce.

For my marks, the Dream is reality. If I choose to kill them there, their body will be found, untouched if I'm careful about my methods, in whatever place I leave it. If I choose to show them pleasures beyond their wildest dreams, they will wake unaware their fantasy had never taken place at all. My gift was a secret known only to one other living person, and it was my greatest weapon in a world where I could claim nothing else to my name.

Stepping close enough to press Mandar's face against my abdomen, I tried to listen for the sound of my bodyguard on the other side of the locked door. Hal was a pathetic protector at best, but when I slipped into the Dream I would be leaving my own body behind for a time. I would be completely vulnerable. If I was disturbed before my mind was ready to disconnect from the host, I would be lost, a soul forever divorced from the body it was meant to inhabit. At least, that was what my grandmother had always said. As it was, Hal could deter people from entering just by telling them who he worked for. No other family in Atlantis could strike fear in the hearts of others the way the Colliers could.

I joined Mandar on his chaise, sliding my body over his until I lay on top of him. I twirled my fingers into what little mousy hair remained on his head. The hazy light made it appear darker than it truly was; or maybe it was just his greasy nature. "Where do you want me?" I asked in a heady whisper, preparing to leave my body.

Mandar squirmed beneath me, his eyes empty of everything but desire. "On your knees."

I blinked my eyes once and I was there, kneeling before him in the very room we had left behind. There were a few differences, there always were, but for a man as unimaginative as Mandar these differences added up to an additional lamp on the nightstand and a mirror on the ceiling over the bed that had replaced the chaise. Even his appearance remained the same. In their Dreams, many men shed unwanted weight, grew back hair long receded, or acknowledged a true gender normally hidden by their subconsciousness. Mandar was simply Mandar, perhaps so sure of himself in life he really didn't need to dream up anything better.

In the Dream I performed as was expected of me, completely subservient for a time, indulging a fantasy or two until he was ripe for the picking. I had never performed any of these acts in my true body. For the most part, I let the man's fantasy guide my actions; my hands on his member twisting just so, as his preferences dictated. Even my ability to feel the pleasure of the act was dependent on whether or not he wanted me to feel it; at least, for the time I let him hold on to his control anyway. There was power in relinquishing control at times. I might have to lay there, staring as blankly as a corpse while he thrust inside me, or as in Mandar's case, just seeing the desire take hold of him could send me into a screaming orgasm. I waited until he was near climax himself, panting and moaning into my chest. Giving Mandar some control at first was necessary if I wanted my lesson to stick.

I waited for the moment when Mandar's control of the Dream was the most relaxed, when he was so sure of his power over me he dared to stroke my hair with something resembling tender gratitude. Then, I took everything from him.

Mandar's eyes bulged when he blinked once to find himself sprawled on the bed, each limb tied to a separate corner by invisible ropes. I left him naked and vulnerable, his belly a slab of fat rolling out to either side of him. His mouth opened to speak but when it did, the very air formed a ball to stop the words preparing to spill forth.

"No, no, no, that's not how this works," I crooned. The sight of him, shaking with rage and fear, made me sick. "You only speak when I tell you to." I made a slow circle of the bed, exchanging my nudity for black slacks and a red sweater that hung lazily off one shoulder. My preferred attire – clothes I could be whipped for possessing in my real life. I leaned over the bed, trapping Mandar with only my eyes. "Now, you should know, Xzan is less than thrilled with you right now. He would like to know why his only son is stuck in Dungeon while you indulge in your depraved fantasies. You can imagine the treatment a young man like Lark might receive there. Or maybe you can't. Should I show you?"

Mandar's mouth strained against the gag until I finally released it. "You bitch! You dare call your master by name."

I was quick to stop his mouth once more. "Did I stutter? I asked you why the son of *your* master is rotting in a cell in Dungeon. What I choose to call the man at the other end of my leash is between me and him."

The sounds escaping Mandar's throat didn't have the quality of someone prepared to act professionally. With a bored sigh, I climbed up onto the bed, straddling Mandar's thick waist. I leaned over to trace a finger down the center of his chest, feeling a small thrill of inner pleasure at the knowledge that I could do anything I wanted, up to and including murder, to the man beneath me. I could see the same awareness start to fill Mandar's eyes. He was thinking the same thing. I filled my face with disappointment, my bottom lip stuck out as I had seen my mistress do when something she fancied was denied her.

"Xzan told me not to kill you," I pouted before letting my face brighten. "In fact, if you want to know, he told me to show you exactly how he prefers to demonstrate his displeasure with those in his employ. It's been a while since I required such punishment myself, but I think I remember it going a bit like this."

The lash falling across Mandar's thighs was invisible; the welts it left were not. I had to tread carefully, marking him just enough to remind him of this lesson in the morning, but not enough for him to recall the Dream too vividly. My role in it was not to be revealed. Ten strikes were standard for a slave who forgot to mind their tongue. Ten was all I gave him. His tender flesh was already threatening to break under the abuse, and the tears trailing down the sides of his face were erasing any pleasure I might have taken in our little role-reversal. When I removed the gag once more, Mandar was suddenly quite willing to discuss the matter at hand.

"Lark killed six people! How was I supposed to keep him out of prison?" he babbled between gasping sobs.

"Well, I'm not the lawyer here, but I should think your typical practice was to bribe a council member or something."

"Your master's son stabbed a pregnant woman eighteen times. He's lucky he's not feeding the beasts of the Wilds as we speak! Dungeon for a few months was the best I could do."

I watched a bead of sweat form in the pit of his scar, my gaze avoiding the terrified hatred seeping out of his beady eyes. In one fluid movement, I swung my leg over to stand next to the bed once more, staring down at the pathetic man in front of me. "I will be sure to tell Xzan everything you have said. I suggest you look into rectifying this mistake of yours. I was told to tell you he expects Lark home within forty-eight hours. He had better be unharmed, or you will be the one feeding the beast of the Wilds."

Mandar's body quivered as he fought the restraints. "What am I supposed to do? There were witnesses! Not to mention that woman was far from a common whore! The Colliers aren't the only powerful family in Atlantis." His voice lost some of its fervor when I made to lean over the side of the bed.

"You poor thing," I crooned, freeing a strand of hair from where it had been stuck to the side of his face by his tears.

Mandar began to whimper. "The Colliers may be the wealthiest family in Atlantis, maybe even the most powerful one, but she was the daughter of someone important, too. What am I supposed to do if everything points to his guilt?"

I sighed, sucking in one corner of my mouth as if I had actually given his words some thought. "I don't know," I shrugged before patting Mandar's cheek. "I guess you have forty-eight hours to figure it out."

Chapter 2

I left Mandar in the Dream, settling back into my own body with a deep sigh. I felt heavier when my mind was confined to my own skin. For Mandar, the punishment I had dealt would seem a well-remembered nightmare; as soon as my mind was fully withdrawn, the Dream would release him. Mandar was a lump of heavy flesh in front of me, snoring softly in true sleep while real dreams floated around harmlessly in his head. With something resembling a pout, I slumped over a little myself. Mandar was a big man and would be difficult to move. As luck would have it, he already lay on the long chaise. Leaving him there would be much easier than dragging him across the room onto his bed.

Undressing took some time though. He wore the typical layers of the free and wealthy. His two light robes were simple to pull off his shoulders, as well as his white linen tunic. With a grunt, I was able to yank each tall boot from his foot before removing his belted skirt and black nylon leggings. In fact, the latter were already half-removed in preparation for the fun he thought he was going to enjoy. Once he was naked, I re-covered him with one of the robes, arranging him as best I could so it would appear as though he had fallen asleep, thoroughly sated.

I gave my appearance a quick assessment in a mirror by the door. Amber eyes stared back at me from a frame of dark lashes which had been accentuated by thick, dark liner. There was a healthy blush to the olive tone of my skin, and my hair was a tousled mess of dark curls from moving Mandar around. I had no tools with which to straighten it back out, but with a few finger strokes and some careful twisting, I got it tied in an adequate knot at the nape of my neck. Xzan expected his property to look pristine at all times. My hands smoothed out my short white skirt and adjusted the white sash that crossed over my breasts. A rebellious urge to smile at my reflection made me hesitate a moment longer. It passed, and I left the room without so much as a flash of straight, white teeth in the mirror.

"That was fast. I guarantee I wouldn't finish so quickly, babe," Hal promised in greeting. He didn't bother looking into the room before the door closed again.

My expression was carefully neutral, a lifetime of practice ensuring my eyes did not so much as flutter in Hal's direction at his implied invitation. As a paid employee, he was as much my superior as Xzan, even if only by a hair. The truth was, as the bodyguard of a slave, he was hardly more than one himself, earning only enough credits to gamble and drink during his free time. To say this irked him would be like saying the sky was blue. I took some comfort from the fact I was an asset to my master, while Hal was a pain in the ass on the verge of looking for new employment as a whipping boy in the fighting pits.

"Don't be such a sourpuss, baby. You might enjoy yourself." Hal gave my rump a good smack before following me down the hallway towards the entrance we had used when we arrived.

"I belong to Xzan," was my only reply, edged with frustration.

Hal made a noise in his throat somewhere between a cough and a grunt. "He doesn't give a shit. I bet if I let him keep my salary for the week, he'd let me take you for the whole night."

"I belong to Xzan."

Usually this was just something to say to keep Hal off my back, however that particular evening I was finding the whole thing highly amusing. Listening to him growl and mutter under his breath gave me back a small sense of the power I had left behind in the Dream. Hal may think he could do as he pleased, "split me down the middle" as he liked to say, but he knew nothing of my true value. Xzan was nothing if not a good businessman, and a true businessman looked out for his investments. I was an investment he had spent many years cultivating for his games of power, not a toy for the likes of Hal to play with.

Outside it was well past midnight on the sixth day of darkness. Our two suns ensured months of daylight at a time. In return, we endured more than two weeks of darkness three or four times a year. As much as I hated the dark, the moon was full and its ghostly light made the tall buildings of the city glow in a haunting sort of way. I admired the jagged edges of its scar – a deep shadow that stretched across its surface like a crack in a pane of glass with a shard missing – giving it the appearance of a growling, white monster. It brightened the sky with its incandescent light. Some saw the gouge left by a stray meteor and considered it an ugly reminder of how close the planet had come to destruction a few short centuries ago; I thought it gave the empty moon a defiant beauty. I envied its audacity. It had saved mankind from extinction and too often we showed our gratitude by lamenting the absence of the suns. There must have been stars out there somewhere, too, lost in the haze of the city lights around us. I had never seen the tiny balls of fire myself, but my grandmother had told me stories of the creatures living among them: the Archer, the Twins, and the Warrior. My imagination created majestic beings racing across an ebony field, chasing the moon or tracking the lost suns. Before Hal could shove me inside the waiting car, I strained to see just one glorious speck of light dancing around the moon. If only the stars had the power to penetrate the darkness the way the moon did; perhaps then my fear would abate during the tedious night.

The car hummed over streets paved only to hide the great magnetic belts which allowed our vehicle to hover gracefully off the ground. I suppose the smooth stone made walking easier on pedestrians as well, but I doubt those who made such decisions cared about the comfort of the common peoples' feet. No. In Atlantis, aesthetics were much more important than practicality. If the two met in one great feat of functionality, well, that was a happy coincidence for all. The fact there were many more pedestrians than hover-cars was beside the point. We were one of the few in a personal vehicle. While I hated how it set us apart from the others still wandering here and there on business better suited to the evening, the curve of my rather uncomfortable stilettos made walking something I avoided; in the comfort of the graceful car, I kept my complaints to myself. I wasn't about to give up so much as an inch of my shoes to assuage the guilt I felt at being the slave of an elite family.

I had earned my place.

I had killed for it.

Most of those we passed were so heavily dressed it was hard to distinguish one face from another. A few street folk scurried out of sight whenever possible, their pitiful rags hardly enough to cover their bodies, let alone their faces. *Their* feet were bare against the cold ground. The poor were always at risk of finding themselves on a slaver's block, stripped of their dignity as well as what clothes they had remaining to them. Slaves were no better than animals, clothed only enough to keep the perversions of the masters in check. The wealthier one was, the more layers of dress one wore, until only the eyes could be seen under the rim of a turban or above a sheer veil. The derelict members of society stayed out of sight whenever possible, trying to live out their lives as invisible as they could. Slaves could be distinguished in the same way. It had been rumoured the servants at the Mayor's house were permitted to wear short dresses, which covered everything from their collarbones to their thighs. A shop owner's slave may wear nothing at all, precious credits saved to clothe the master's family first. My toes curled against the confines of my shoes when I watched a woman dart into a building, followed quickly by a young boy wearing nothing but the mop of shaggy dark hair on his head.

I shivered.

"Want me to keep you warm?"

The smell of smoke filled the cab. The acrid taste of it stung my lungs, causing my mind to drift away from my body before I gathered enough wits to pull it back. Hal was lucky enough to inhale the drug and feel nothing more than the mellow high of total relaxation. Our driver was only a hologram, meant to comfort passengers who were uneasy trusting their lives to an autopilot system. Essentially, we were completely alone. Hal's hand found a place to rest on my thigh, his thumb making small circles as it inched closer to the hem of my skirt. I struggled to find clean air to breathe, but when I didn't reply to his offer, my bodyguard blew the *ghanja* into my face.

"I am Xzan's," I coughed, one hand coming up to protect my mouth and nose. My head began to spin.

"No, no, just relax. Enjoy yourself for once," Hal laughed, tugging my hand away from my face with his in the same motion he used to slide the other one the rest of the way up my leg. I squirmed to get away; he interpreted the motion as desire for more. "That's right, baby. I don't know why Xzan wastes you on all those johns. If he isn't gonna bother keeping you to himself, do you really think he'll mind if I have a taste?" His breath was hot in my ear before he trailed a series of kisses down my neck.

Anger swelled beneath my breast until I could feel it blazing from my eyes. Lifting them slowly, I pulled away to look up into Hal's. They were blue. I had never been at liberty to notice until now. Hal seemed to like my sudden forward behaviour, so I took a serious risk. I launched myself onto his lap to gaze into their icy depths as deeply as I could. The *ghanja* was loosening my hold on my temper, allowing the rage to take on a life of its own. The window to everybody's soul exists in the eyes.

When I found his, already wedged open by the smoke and his own unbridled lust, I sent tendrils of desire spilling in.

"You want to have me, Hal." I let his name float off my tongue, my voice offering as much promise as my hips moving against his pelvis. "You want to split me down the middle and show me what only a real woman could ask for." I watched his head nod, bobbing my head in a similar motion until I knew he was losing himself to the rhythm. I reached my hands up to close his eyes with my fingers. Leaning in close I whispered in his ear. "Where do you want me?"

When I leaned back, we were in my world. The Dream. We were in a room I had created for myself, a room just for these occasions. The inferno of my anger sparkled in the air, wresting control from the rational side of me. I had no means, or real desire, to stop what happened next. I was still straddling Hal, only now he was the one in a slave's skirt and no shirt to hide the bulky muscles of his arms and chest. He looked around, confused by the white walls draped with hanging strings of lights. He was lying flat on a long table, the cold metal no doubt biting into his skin. He tried to sit up, but I pushed him back down with only a finger.

"What is this?" he demanded, showing far more fear than Mandar had at the sight of me in control. I soaked it up.

"This is what you wanted, right? To play the game so many of those johns have played before," I held up a long-bladed knife that had appeared out of thin air, its silver hilt glittering in the bright lights of the room. Hal's eyes widened. I trailed the tip of the blade along the skin between his pecs, watching as a thin line of red bloomed like butterfly wings beneath its touch. "I'm going to show you what really goes on while you stand guard outside the door."

His screams echoed off the walls.

His blood painted them red.

Chapter 3

I awoke disoriented. My eyes fluttered open while blurred images came hesitantly into focus. I realized I was at home, in my own room and on my own bed. My head was spinning, bringing a wave of nausea over me too overwhelming to swallow back. I hardly made it across the room to my toilet before spewing what little contents my stomach contained into the metal bowl. Once I was able to catch my breath, I sat heavily on the floor, waiting for the throbbing in my head to abate. The *ghanja* smoke had made the trip to the Dream a dangerous one. I couldn't even remember how I had found my way back into my own body. It still didn't feel like a good fit, like wearing oversized shoes that slipped with each step I took. My eyes travelled across the tiny cubicle I was fortunate enough to have all to myself. My bed was within arm's reach so I crawled back onto it, longing for a large quilt to burrow under. I settled for the thin sheet I was permitted to ward off the chill of an empty room. *It's probably warmer in the slave quarters,* I groaned inwardly, picturing the other men and women at least able to hold each other for warmth and comfort. The thought made me long for my grandmother. Too many years separated my memories from the reality of her touch.

The speaker by my door buzzed to life. "Xzan's office. Ten minutes."

Ten minutes. Enough time to clean the vomit from my chin and properly smooth out my hair. I could not move quickly enough to change my clothes. My limbs betrayed me in their inability to perform the tasks my mind asked them to do. *Foolish,* I reprimanded myself as my soul tried to settle deeper into its proper host. When my door slid open to let me leave my room, all I could really do was ensure my skirt was straight and the ties at the back of my neck, holding my sash in place, had not come loose.

Outside of my room there was no one waiting to escort me. I turned down the empty corridor, studiously ignoring the barren metallic walls by keeping my eyes lowered as would be expected. When I approached my personal door to Xzan's office, I waved my hand over the scanner just above the door handle. A subtle *ting* sounded from within to acknowledge my accepted blood-scent, before the door slid into itself to allow me through. I was the only one outside the family whose genetic code was programmed into the security features of the house. It gave me less freedom than the honour would suggest, but then, every little shred of decency I could get was a precious gem I coveted in a life of nothing.

With the deepest breath I could gather, I stepped inside my master's office. My heart raced with more than a touch of fear.

Xzan sat at his desk. His head was bowed over a holograph messenger, speaking too low for me to hear. With a wave of a long-fingered hand, Xzan dismissed the image. It was then that he noticed me waiting. I was quick to avert my eyes, having been caught observing him openly, but he chuckled patiently, as though he had caught an impertinent child sneaking into the office. My eyes travelled as high as his baby-smooth chin, too narrow to be considered a feature of strength. Still, a single word from those pursed lips would see the fool who called it weak strung from the city walls. I was no fool.

"I'm told Hal had an unfortunate accident on the way home last night," he paused, circling around his desk to stand in front of me. Booted feet crossed themselves as he leaned back on his desk. "Not a mark on him. If it hadn't been for the autopsy performed, for insurance reasons of course, we might have just assumed he smoked enough *ghanja* to have simply died in his sleep. Although, he *did* die in his sleep, I suppose. Do you want to know what the poor soul who examined his corpse found?"

This wasn't a question, no matter what inflection he added to the end of the sentence. I set my teeth to stop my lip from trembling.

Xzan went on, pushing himself away from the desk to walk around me. Every step echoed off the empty walls of his office and brought a fresh wave of goosebumps to my flesh. "His insides had been sliced to ribbons. His death was ruled inconclusive in the end, but that poor fellow who examined dear Hal, well, he informed me it was as if a rather large animal had tried to claw its way out from the inside." He paused, standing before me once more. My knees started to shake. "Look at me and explain yourself."

"Master I –" A solid blow across my face knocked the rest of the words from my lips before I could even raise my head to meet his eyes. I lifted a hand to touch my nose, pulling it away to see the bright crimson of blood on my palm. My fingers explored it further until I felt assured it wasn't broken. Xzan would never willfully damage property in such a way. I straightened, attempting to follow through in the command I had already been given, but another strike sent me to the floor. My tongue tentatively felt my teeth; none seemed loose. I knew he was still holding back, even if there were bright spots of light dancing in my vision.

Xzan knelt down, reaching his hand out to stroke my hair. Somehow, I managed not to flinch. "Such a silly little girl," he crooned until I managed to look up into his eyes. They were a soft brown, almost trustworthy if you didn't know the man they belonged to; the hard features of a slender face were softened by sympathy. "You know I have cameras in my cars. Hal would have been punished for his behaviour. Touching another man's slave in such a way is certainly worth a good lashing. Touching one of *my* slaves may even have seen him sold to the fighting pits. You had not been given the authority to pass judgement in my name. Now I can hardly punish you publicly, it would raise too many questions, but you will be punished. After all, it took a small fortune to shut the mouth of the medical examiner."

Xzan continued to stroke my head until he was convinced I would not dissemble. Then, his reprimand complete, he stood and straightened out the knee length black robe he wore around the house. "Go stand in the corner until I tell you otherwise."

I obeyed as slowly as I dared, resisting the urge to wipe the blood from my face though it had begun to drip onto the pristine white of my skirt. The corner he referred to was one of two behind his desk. In both were two low pedestals scarcely wide enough for me to stand with my feet together. I was lucky. I was small enough to balance there for hours, though my back and feet would soon protest. I had seen two male slaves, their hands and feet bound, made to stand there as punishment for trying to flee. Their feet had hung over the sharp edges, bleeding onto the floor until at last one fell, freeing them both from the slow torture. My ability to stand there felt like a righteous "Fuck you!" to the man now flicking his fingers through the air above his desk while various files manifested before him.

I hadn't eaten, or had anything to drink for that matter, since the afternoon before. The resulting dizziness made my resolution to stand tall begin to waver. Not only was the world slowly spinning out of focus, my pedestal had grown too slippery to maintain my balance. I looked down, surprised to see I must have cut myself on the edge. I didn't recall any pain, but the small pool of blood caused my feet to slide away from each other. *I will not fall,* I thought fiercely, gathering my wits to hold myself together. I would not give Xzan the satisfaction.

I focused instead on broken memories.

My mother had been taken from my life before my skin could create a memory of her touch. They say no one in Atlantis dies of disease, and physical deformities have long since been corrected through genetic modifications, but my mother wasn't a true Atlantian, so I suppose the rules didn't apply to her. My grandmother had been taken from the Wilds outside the city, a pregnant girl sold to the highest bidder on the slaver's block. I'm not sure when Xzan acquired her, but I do know it was my mother he had truly been after.

As my grandmother would tell me later, my gift was a gift from my ancestors. The true people of this world. They had chosen to live in harmony with their planet, while those in Atlantis strove only to overcome it. Centuries had separated the cultures until the Wilds became uninhabitable, and the only Wilders left had been enslaved. How Xzan had known my bloodline carried the gift he needed I would never know, but he spared no thought to the woman who had bled to death bringing me into this world. I had long since learned she could have been saved, but having suffered the heartache of losing my grandmother, I decided it was better to lose a stranger I had no memory of than the mother she might have been.

As I fought a new wave of dizziness, I pictured the soft lines of my grandmother's face and told myself one of her stories:

The Twins were the most beautiful beings in this world. They were neither man nor woman, yet somehow both at the same time. They were tall and lean, and their dark eyes mesmerized humanity and showed them the infinite possibilities of the galaxy. They were there the day our people and the people of Atlantis parted ways. Before our histories could diverge, they offered us all a warning.

"If you continue down this path, your world will face certain destruction. The planet will wilt and die, the oceans will turn to poison and swallow you all."

The Atlantians laughed and built their walls taller. They mined the ores from the ground to make their walls stronger. No ocean would ever swallow them, and they created great factories where food could be created so the death of the planet need never bother them. Our people, we tried to keep the world alive. We nurtured the growing things and protected every living creature we found. We tried to keep the world alive, but we failed.

The Twins, seeing humanity choose its doom, left our world to join the stars in the sky. They watch over us even now, but they will not stop the world from ending. When Atlantis learns its lesson, there will be no second chances.

From my pedestal in the corner, I glared at the fine white strands that glittered in Xzan's hair. While I stood there, all sensation lost in my weeping feet, I hoped I would be there to watch my master face the final lesson we were promised.

Chapter 4

At last, Xzan stood from his desk. He stretched out tight muscles in his lower back before leaving the room. He did not so much as glance in my direction. Remembering his cameras, I stayed where I was. Minutes stretched themselves out until I thought hours must have passed. Just as I was beginning to sag against one wall, another slave-woman came in through the same door I had used to enter the office, and I was permitted to collapse into her arms.

She had no name that I knew of. If any slave had a name, it was only the ones we created for ourselves in our minds. I called her Red, to acknowledge the fiery colour of her hair. I thought she was a maid. She would often visit my chambers to clean my toilet or bring me fresh clothes. Because she was so rarely seen by anyone beyond our household, she was permitted to wear a full white tunic, belted at the waist, and a white skirt that reached all the way to the floor. It was an honour for her to be dressed so well, as well as a sign that she could be relied on to do her job. Her only failure was her battle against time. She'd been around at least ten years longer than my twenty-five years, and gravity was already pulling at the soft skin of her face. Xzan would not keep her much longer even if she did work in obedient silence. Though she had been around as long as I could remember, there were no slaves kept in the Collier home who might be called old by any means. I had heard it said that Mrs. Collier disliked the reminder that her own beauty was quickly fading into memory. It seemed no genetic modification could stop the flow of time.

In the moments I sat in her presence, as she gently cleaned off my face and helped me change into fresh garments, I decided I would miss Red when our Master decided she no longer fit the aesthetics of his home. As soon as I had acknowledged the future sense of loss, I tucked it away in my heart to keep it safe from anyone who might notice my weakness. For Red, I hardly managed a smile; her impending loss already hurt too much. Once I was clean and presentable again, Red passed me a few ENSA cubes before moving to clean off the pedestal.

I held the food in my hands for a minute to grimace at their bland appearance. These ones had no artificial colour added to enhance their appeal, so instead of something I might consume for sustenance, it was as if I had been handed four metal building blocks to play with. I remembered seeing an advertisement for the cubes as a child. Smiling people had been popping cubes of every colour in their mouth as words like "strawberry pie" and "mashed potatoes and gravy" appeared over their heads. Enhanced Nourishment and Sustenance Aliments were the answer to the question nobody had asked: how long before the fish farms and greenhouses could no longer support a city of millions now that the rest of the planet was dead? A decade later, and the greenhouses and fish farms could barely support the luxurious demands of the wealthiest Atlantians, let alone anyone else.

I chewed the first cube slowly, not trusting its colourless lack of appeal even though I scarcely remembered anything else. Instinct insisted this was not what food was meant to be. There were stories of a time before the wall surrounding Atlantis was built – before the moon had defended our world with its own celestial mass from an onslaught of space rock, and figures in the stars still walked among us – that food had grown fresh and bountiful from the earth. The sea yielded all manner of creatures for human consumption, and the Wilds boasted all manner of beasts that could provide meat for a master's table. Such days were long gone, lost to memory and myth. The little ENSA cubes we ate now were made in a lab, filled with synthetic vitamins to keep us healthy and designed to fool our minds into thinking we were feasting as our ancestors had.

When Atlantis learns its lesson, there will be no second chances. My grandmother's voice in my head made me shiver.

Though I still eyed the two other cubes with distrust, the flavour from the first one exploded on my tongue and warmed me from the inside out when I swallowed. The sensation of wrongness passed, and I indulged a small smile. *Tomato soup,* I sighed. I popped the next colourless cube into my mouth with the same lucky result. The third cube was something sweet, with the soft sting of cinnamon; I didn't know what it was called, but I was sure Red had snuck it among the other two as a treat just for me. By the time I had swallowed all three, I was satiated and more than a little grateful. Red passed me a cup of water with a small, secret smile of her own. I looked deep into her clear blue eyes, wishing my gift would let me thank her without words. Perhaps I could sneak into her dreams later to tell her properly. I had never tried to invade someone's sleep before, but I had never wished for anything more fervently.

For now, our silent exchange seemed to be enough.

Just as Xzan was returning from his own meal, Red was disappearing through the servants' door. She took the filth of the morning with her. I stood on my pedestal, trying not to glare triumphantly at the man now staring proudly at my corner as if I were a piece of art he had recently acquired.

Fuck you, I screamed inside. Outwardly, I stood a little straighter.

Thomas

Thomas watched his brother Jack where he sat proudly atop the painted warhorse, and his nails bit into the soft flesh of his palms. The young man in the saddle, its high cantle aptly hiding the softening midsection of the newly raised member of the court, raised his hand. The light caught a freshly minted gauntlet, sending spots of light into Thomas' eyes; he refused to raise his hand to shield against it. The proud animal carrying all that pomp had its black coat spoiled by obnoxious splashes of red and green; it snorted and stomped as if to share in Thomas' bitterness. Why must such a noble creature suffer the weight of someone so unworthy? The bells and metal armour weighing down both the saddle and the embroidered blankets caused a raucous clatter in tandem with iron shoes against the cobblestones. The stud's ears flicked back in annoyance at its own commotion. When they passed by where Thomas was standing among the other on-lookers, Jack's eyes passed right over his brother's head as if he were no more than another member of the rabble. The animal felt the animosity in the crowd, tasted it with each flare of his nostrils, and nearly pranced on top of the youth from which so many negative emotions came. I should be yours, *the stud seemed to say.*

You should be mine, *Thomas had to agree.*

It was too late now. His own chance to right the wrong was gone. There were some who knew the truth, who had witnessed Thomas' deeds and praised him for his courage and wit. But where were they now? He thought about leaping in front of the lords and ladies, the merchants, and the peasants. He thought about pulling Jack from the saddle and taking his place. He would scream above the crowd "It was me! I saved you all!" and it would be Thomas who slept in a lord's castle for the rest of his days. Except, even in his mind, he could hear the disbelieving laughter of the onlookers who now cheered for their false hero.

Blunderdore had been the second one to fall to Thomas' sturdy hatchet. What had started as a second attempt to show his worthiness in the eyes of the villagers was stolen once more by his brother's interference. As it turned out, it was too unbelievable that a mere boy could beat a giant; a wimp of a boy at that. The sturdy Jack, who had been building up a husky exterior that would one day turn to fat, was by far the more attractive hero. At nine-years old, sometimes even Thomas couldn't believe he had defeated two great brutes at all.

Thomas went back to his imagination. "It was me, you fools! Me! I slew the mighty Blunderdore while Jack pissed his pants where he had been hung from a peg on the wall." It wouldn't work. He had tried once, after Ol' Blunder had met his end.

Five years later things were different. He was growing quickly and more than ready to prove his worth to Arthur and all those prissy knights in their shiny armour. How many of their deeds were written in the blood of pages or squires? The bitterness was too much for Thomas to bear any longer.

Soon, he wouldn't have to.

While his brother rode off to his new estates, his banner catching the wind to proudly display the image of the headless giant he had so recently bested, Thomas turned away from the procession and lost himself in the wheat-fields bordering the side of the road. The tiny treasures in his pocket tingled through the coarse fabric of his breeches, feeding the frenzy in his soul.

The last giant had been little more than a boy. A seven-foot tall boy, with arms the size of oak trees and a voice meant to send shivers through the earth when he spoke, but a boy none-the-less. He hadn't needed to die. Thomas' scowl deepened at the memory of it.

Jack had told Thomas the lady had been kidnapped, that she had been enchanted by the giant to make her love him. It had been a lie. The sound of her heart shattering at the sight of Thomas, soaked in the giant's life-blood, echoed around his head like wind wailing through the trees. If he had known, if Jack had bothered to tell his little brother about the real power of the gem now pinned to his new bride's collar, Thomas would have done things differently. Now the lady truly was enchanted. She would spend the rest of her life with a real monster. A giant of a different kind, Thomas mused, considering Jack's swollen ego.

The towering wheat – the stalks rustled against his ears in a way that usually brought a sense of calm, like listening to the steady fall of rain outside a window, but instead only seemed to match the way his blood thundered in his ears – gave way to a murky creek bed, all but dried up save for the hideous brown water slogging through rivets in the mud. Thomas remembered leaping what seemed like a terrifying river as a child. He had laughed over his shoulder at Jack, six years the elder, huddling on the bank like a terrified toddler. The memory churned inside his gut, driving the force of his leap to the far side. Maybe the creek had always been so shallow and pathetic. Perhaps it was the way things worked as one left behind their childhood: perceptions changed until what was once a mighty mountain became no more than a molehill bent on tripping a weary traveler. A small part of Thomas hoped this was not true. He lived under the shroud of anger and regret he had been building up since he caught that first giant, since he had watched in muted horror as Jack took the credit for a deed he would never have been able to do on his own. Though the memory was a stain on the joy of childhood, somewhere deep inside his soul Thomas knew there was happiness out there waiting for him.

The far side of the creek bed served as a resting place for a great boulder, partially buried in the ground. A shallow crevice, smoothed out by many a passing traveler before, made the perfect place for Thomas to collapse under the weight of his thoughts. He paused for a breath, running a hand over his head. In one smooth motion, his hand untangled itself from a lock of tawny hair to dive into his pocket and grip the treasures within.

He brought his fist out in front of him, wrapping his free hand around it as if afraid the magic he held might burst forth. When he relaxed his grasp, each finger unfurling one at a time, it was almost a disappointment to see the three small stones resting against his palm. They were a pale green, with veins of silver coursing through them, like small pebbles of marble. They were beans, shaped like any other bean Thomas had ever seen, yet he could feel them buzzing excitedly against his skin. Let us fly, they begged. A breeze tickled the base of Thomas' neck, tossing the beans in little circles in his hand. Thomas made more of an effort to shelter them with his other hand.

Let us fly.

Guilt forced him to close his fist once more. The giant, who had had a name though Thomas refused to remember it, had shown the beans to the friendly youth who had been invited to dinner. They were supposed to be his ticket home. He would wed the beautiful maiden – who had grown to love what others called a beast – and take her to the land he came from. A land in the clouds where they could live without fear of Jack the Giant Slayer. Thomas had kept a straight face, nodding his head while his hand gripped his sword beneath the table. The giant had spent a lifetime searching for these beans. Now they belonged to Thomas. Now he would be the one to find a place to be free of Jack's shadow.

Before he could give in to hesitation, Thomas threw the beans down into the creek bed and watched them sink into the mud. He imagined he felt the earth shutter in its desire to consume the magic it had been offered. For one agonizing moment after another, nothing happened. Thomas cursed the giant for filling his head with fancy, then banged the heel of his boot off the boulder only to curse again at the burst of pain shooting through his ankle.

Thomas was getting to his feet when he realized how still the earth had become. There was an absence of sound like he had never experienced before. His ears felt as though they had been stuffed with rags. The air was too thick to breathe. His eyes darted this way and that, searching for some clue to tell him he was still in his own land. A few yards to his left, a hawk was diving towards the ground, its unsuspecting prey locked in sight. Normal. Everything was as it should be. That is, until Thomas realized the bird was not diving at all. It had been. Its glassy talons were outstretched and ready to grab whatever poor creature lay out of sight among the tall grass. Its wings were frozen in their vertical position, snowy feathers exposed. Even as Thomas tried to understand the raptor's position in the air, an explosion tore the earth apart around him.

While everything else remained locked in place, something was growing where the beans had sunk into the earth. It was a beanstalk. Its enormous foliage unfurled like stairs as the behemoth green snake shot into the heavens. Thomas lost himself in his own shocked terror, barely able to raise his arms to shield his eyes against the dirt filling the air. He was as frozen as that hawk, his quarry right before his eyes but he could not yet reach out to grab it. The deafening roar was too painful to bear. Thomas fell to his knees, shoving his fists against his ears while his own screams melted into the chaos.

As suddenly as it had begun, it all ended. The hawk, its momentum interrupted by the appearance of the beanstalk rising up into the clouds, veered sharply back into the skies to re-affirm its reign there. Thomas opened eyes that were previously squeezed shut to stare at what he had summoned forth. One sturdy leaf was resting against the riverbank as if beckoning him to take that first step towards a greater destiny. Though his knees shook, Thomas managed to get to his feet. He wiped bits of earth from the sleeves of his shirt while he eyed the leafy staircase in front of him. All the courage for which his brother was known burned within Thomas' chest, building upon the certainty he was following the right path. He gathered this confidence into himself, stepping onto the leaf and shedding all doubt. Somewhere overhead, beyond the distant expanse of blue, was the promise of adventure. One step after another, Thomas grinned at the sheer pleasure of meeting whatever destiny might decide to hand him.

Chapter 5

The door to the office buzzed once. Xzan waved his hand over a screen to see who was waiting on the other side. A holographic-Mandar stood there, wringing his hands in the oversized cuffs of his sleeves. His eyes kept darting up at the camera despite his efforts to look straight ahead. Even with the soft blue haze of the image, I could see the sheen of sweat on the lawyer's face; the scar on his forehead looked like a scraggy wart. Xzan glanced to where I still stood on my bloodied pedestal, silently telling myself another of my grandmother's stories to keep from falling. My feet and legs had grown numb after standing several more hours while Xzan went about his business.

"You must have done a number on him," Xzan chuckled under his breath before he pressed the icon to open the door. Before the real Mandar could step fully into the room, Xzan had cleared his desk and arranged his face into an expression of frigid rage. At the sight of my master, Mandar tripped over the hem of his robes.

"Mr. Collier," he bobbed his head up and down, eyes bulging with the same fear I had induced in the Dream. "I'm sorry to disturb you sir. I just – I wanted to give you the good news in person. About your son, that is."

"You mean the one who has been rotting away in Dungeon for almost a week?" Xzan's voice sent a chill through the room that made my knees tremble even despite my self-control. "Please, what good news do you bring?"

Mandar had to swallow several times to find the words. "Ah yes, well, you see, there seems to have been a mix up. New witnesses, you see. Ones who claim to have seen someone else at the club that night. Another man who fought with Ms. Joplin and followed her home. So, you see, Mr. Collier, your son must be innocent after all." Despite his trembling jowls, Mandar managed a weak smile.

I wondered how much these new witnesses had cost. Or had they been paid at all? A forgiven debt could be just as powerful as a favour owed.

Xzan bit his top lip as if weighing the quality of the news he was hearing, his hands steepled in front of him. "This is indeed good news; my wife will certainly be pleased to hear it, even if I remain less than impressed by the quality of your service these past few weeks. My opinion of you seems destined to deteriorate as I'm afraid we have yet another problem." His hands separated and came together again with a clap. Mandar jumped at the sound. "I was kind enough to send you one of my girls for payment last night. She was to your satisfaction, I presume?"

Mandar's eyes slithered over to me. I winked before giving him the hint of a smile, then enjoyed some silent laughter when he sputtered through his answer. "Yes, sir. It was a pleasant evening. I am quite grateful for your generosity."

"Good," Xzan replied firmly. "Except, I am afraid there was an unfortunate accident on the way home. A trusted employee – you understand how hard those are to come by – was killed. Now, you can hardly be held accountable for *accidents,* but I can't help but wonder that if I hadn't been so generous with my slave, Hal might still be alive today."

"Mr. Collier, sir, I'm not sure I understand." The scar on Mandar's head scrunched up into a quivering speck. It annoyed me for some reason, but I was grateful for the distraction a little superiority provided.

"It seems to me, Mr. Fork, that you have been a part of a somewhat disappointing chapter of my life: my son going to jail while under your representation, my best bodyguard succumbing to some strange affliction moments after leaving your home." Xzan leaned forward, his dark eyes penetrating Mandar's very soul almost as aptly as I could. "I greatly dislike leaving my business deals on such a sour note. Don't you?"

Mandar began to wring his hands again, his eyes darting around while he thought of something to say. "Perhaps, sir, perhaps...That is to say." His face lit up for a moment. "Perhaps I might be able to remedy your staffing problem."

"Go on."

Mandar swallowed a small measure of his fear at Xzan's feigned interest. "A new slave, sir. I just bought him last week. Forty thousand credits, if you can believe it, sir, but worth every one of them. He's strong and well-bred. The perfect bodyguard, and you don't even have to pay him. He is waiting for me downstairs if you want to see him, sir."

I watched Xzan tap his chin while he considered it. Slaves for bodyguards were not unheard of, but they rarely showed the same loyalty as a free man trying to earn a paycheck. Finally, Xzan placed a hand on his desk. "Send in Mr. Fork's slave."

"Right away, sir," a disembodied voice replied.

I had been feeling better since indulging in the ENSA cubes Red had provided, but even so it was difficult not to fidget where I stood. A cramp was forming in my left calf, and it was only a matter of time before it sent me to the floor. The only satisfaction I could take from my presence was the way Mandar pointedly avoided looking at me. The pleasure I had given him in the Dream was remembered as real, but the threats tied off in his psyche were like a bad feeling he couldn't quite shake. He likely thought them no more than a nightmare. A very vivid nightmare, complete with subtle red stripes across his thighs when he awoke in the morning. No doubt the moment he saw them, he felt the memory of a threat and made the appropriate phone calls. It was actually quite impressive to see him here already; a job well done. If I could have, I might have given myself a pat on the back.

When the door buzzed to admit Mandar's guard, I found myself unable to keep from staring openly at the specimen that entered the room. The man was taller than any I had ever seen before, towering over Xzan when he stood to examine him. The slave wore a belted white kilt as many of us did, and nothing else. His arms, his legs, even his chest, were carved out in smooth, defined muscles, moving with a fluid grace when he walked across the room. I had never seen a wild cat in person, yet seeing this man here before me, I knew such creatures must be real. There was something different about his presence, the fluidity of his movements, that screamed predator. While others may have shrunk in fear, I could not quite stop myself from leaning toward him as though drawn to his magnetism. After all, to most men I was anything but prey. The way he dominated the room, even in the face of Xzan's authority, was a sight to behold. No one who stepped in at that moment would presume to say the slave was not there by choice.

Despite the visible signs of strength, he was lithe, almost slender, his broad shoulders giving way to a narrow waist. He was hairy, too, like someone had decided he was more animal than man and neglected to laser away the excess body hair as the rest of us had had done shortly after puberty hit. Curling golden hair decorated his chest and made a fine line to follow below where the kilt allowed me to see. With an uncharacteristic blush, I forced my eyes higher again. I was startled to catch his gaze on me. His eyes were green, with flecks of gold to match the tawny hair curling around his ears. *Unkempt.* I vaguely heard Xzan's observation, unable to look away from the haunted expression I saw before me. Those eyes were hollow. There was no glimmer of life in them, and not even the hint of a soul. I was mesmerized.

"He was a fighter before I bought him. Slavers found him wandering in the Wilds as a youth, I'm told. They trained him for the ring, and he killed every man he came up against."

Xzan made a second full circle before stopping in front of the stoic man before him. "If he was a winner, why did they sell him at all? Are there defects?" He raised the front of the kilt, assuring himself the slave was intact. An arched brow was the only indication my master was impressed by what he saw. I couldn't help sneaking a satisfied peek as well. "If nothing else he'd make a good breeder."

The slave glared down at Xzan, his mouth set in a grim line. Xzan met the glare with carefully concealed outrage. "He's not even trained properly. How do you propose to keep a brute like this under control?"

"With this," Mandar produced a collar from somewhere in the layers of his clothing. It was a slender metal band which Mandar promptly reached up to clasp around his slave's neck. I had seen such devices before, on runaways mostly. Once there, only the genetic scent of the owner would be able to remove it. It could track the wearer anywhere, sending jolts of electricity at the touch of a button. Mandar handed the remote over. "I've never had to use it myself. He's a surly fellow, but he is also obedient."

"Hmmm." Xzan glared at the man before him. "Kneel!" He commanded.

The slave lowered himself to one knee, finally allowing Xzan to glare down at him properly. His knee had hardly touched the floor, when Xzan held down the button on the remote for a count of three. The slave's back arched once before he fell to his side, spasming. When the current was released, he silently returned to the kneeling position, his glare appropriately downcast.

"Next time, I expect you to respond more quickly," Xzan told him. He turned to Mandar who had blanched at the sight of the slave's lesson. "I will take the insolent beast off your hands, Mandar. You can consider our business done."

Mandar couldn't hide his relief. "Thank you, sir. I will send the release papers for your son immediately."

As soon as the lawyer was out of the room, Xzan finally acknowledged me still standing resolutely in the corner. "Come," he commanded, his voice dripping with feigned kindness. When I obeyed - I was forgiven my slow response as I stepped forward on damaged feet - he made a show of running a hand over my head while he looked down at the tawny head bent before him. "You see how you are supposed to behave?"

The man kneeling before us glanced up, but I couldn't meet his eyes even if I had wanted to. Shame flooded every inch of me, standing as I was next to our master. It was a strange and troubling sensation.

"Here's how this is going to work," Xzan informed us, twirling the remote in his hand while he spoke. "You are going to protect her with your life when you are not protecting me. It took me years to breed her, and she is worth more to me than a hundred of you. Do you understand?"

The man on his knees nodded, his eyes still cast downward. Xzan dipped his head to acknowledge his own satisfaction before his hand moved away from my skull. "Well, as luck would have it, there is a spare cell next to yours," he spoke to me now. "Take him there, then return to your own room."

I bowed my head. "Yes, master."

The tall man stood and followed me from the office. I led him down the narrow corridor, absently wondering if his shoulders touched the sides but too nervous to look behind me to see. At my own door, I paused.

"This is my room," I said, keeping my voice low enough not to be caught by the cameras in the hall. "Yours is there." I pointed to the next door.

Hesitation held me a moment longer, allowing me to look up at his intriguing eyes once more. Maybe there was a soul in there after all. It stared back at me from where it hid behind the shadows of terrible memories. I wondered if anyone else had ever noticed the profound sorrow I could see echoed in their depths. Before I could say anything to bring more punishment down on me, I turned to walk away.

"The masters in the pits called me Wilder, but my real name is Thomas."

Startled, I spun to look at the other slave once more. Though his eyes were still sad, there was the slightest twitch at the corner of his mouth. I imagined it was a carefully concealed smile. "Slaves don't have names," I told him firmly. "Especially not names as strange as yours."

His lips twitched again. "I wasn't always a slave. In my land, my name is about as common as a name can be." The way the words danced off his tongue, curling at the ends like a song, made me want to hear him speak some more. *Where is your land?* I wanted to ask.

"Slaves aren't supposed to speak to each other either," I replied carefully, all too aware how much I wanted to keep talking.

"I've always found that to be a rule the masters don't often enforce."

I wanted to smile, to be amused by his casual dismissal of those who held our lives in their hands, but I couldn't. "Not here," I told him, glancing pointedly up at the camera pointing directly at us. "Xzan will not tolerate it. Have you ever seen a tongue cut from a person's mouth?"

"Yes, I have," Thomas said, a mask falling over the amusement in his expression. We stood in silence, neither one sure what to say next. Thomas made the next observation. "You speak *his* name," he pointed out. "Does the master tolerate *that?*"

"I'm already in trouble today," I replied with a hint of humour crinkling the corners of my eyes. "I killed my last bodyguard not twenty-four hours ago, which ranks a little higher on the list of things I may be reprimanded for. He didn't follow the rules, so I disemboweled him."

I turned before Thomas could see the smile on my face. His sudden reassessment of my value amused me. My door opened at my approach, but before I went inside, I looked back at the strange man. He still watched me, though his face was unreadable.

"I had a name once, too," I told him, taking the first step into my room. "I was called Xzya. Although, I remember my grandmother used to call me her little nightshade when she thought the master wasn't listening."

"Belladonna," Thomas nodded, using a term I had never heard before. My breath caught in my throat when his teeth were revealed by a genuine smile. "Sounds appropriate. Where I'm from, belladonna is often used as a poison. *The beautiful death,* some call it."

"There is no beauty in death," I said before disappearing into my room.

Laying on my bed, I wondered about the word he had used. *Belladonna.* I had never heard it before, yet it felt right. Nightshade extract could help a person sleep for an hour or a lifetime, just as I could. *Belladonna.* I rolled the name around in my head, closing my eyes to picture the flower I had only ever heard described before. It was strange to think I had a name someone might actually use. It made me happy to think I had had one all along, hidden in the whispers of my grandmother's voice. *Sleep well, my little nightshade.* And for what remained of the day I did just that.

Chapter 6

I slept through the night, enjoying the strangest dreams I had ever experienced before. I was in the Wilds, though what I saw was nothing like what I had glimpsed over the walls of the city as a child. Instead of slogging through sandy dunes, I was walking through stalks of grass tall enough to tickle the palms of my outstretched hands. The sunlight on my skin was a warm caress; I looked up to see only one golden orb hanging lazily in a blue sky that stretched beyond the horizon. I had never seen such a clear sky before, as if the cotton white clouds were scrubbing it clean as they danced in slow motion on the breeze. The sensation of eyes following my progress through the meadow pricked the back of my neck, but a lack of privacy was so much a part of my waking life I hardly gave the feeling credence. I felt no threat in this strange land. Even the air on my face was refreshingly real: cool and crisp and without the metal tang of the city polluting the senses. Spinning with my face turned up to the lonely sun, I tried to take in every detail so I could form such a place in the Dream.

I awoke feeling something akin to what I imagined happiness might be like, so I ran to my mirror to see what effect it had on my features. My lips curved up at the corners. The smile was so imperceptible others may not even notice the change it made to my features, but I could feel that smile in every cell of my body like the echo of an electrical current after a shock. I hummed to myself while I prepared for my day, lingering over each brushstroke if only to be sure the smile wouldn't fade too quickly. In my good mood, I also admired the inky, blue sheen of my hair and the smooth olive complexion of my skin. If I closed my eyes, I could almost imagine that the song on my lips and the soft tug of the brush against my hair was the ghost of my grandmother inhabiting my body.

Thinking of her chased the remnants of my happy dream away and my smile with it.

Just as I was tucking the last of my wayward curls into a twisted bun on top of my head, I heard Thomas' door open and close. I waited for a sign that my own door would open as well. The click of heels passed by my room, but their echo faded without my door sliding into the wall. When it remained sealed shut, I returned to the usual morning routine of my everyday life with a sigh that briefly fogged up my mirror. I held my makeup pod to each eye, blinking once after the pre-programmed application was complete. I was ready for whatever might be required for the day. There was nothing else for me to do until I was summoned, so I returned to sit on my bed. As I leaned against the wall I now shared with Thomas, I wondered – not for the first time – if I might not be in Dungeon as much as my master's son was.

Thomas.

I had never met a slave with a name I hadn't made up in my head before. I pondered it for a while. Pets were given names. Even the ones that scratched furniture or took a shit on the living room floor had names with which their master could lovingly admonish them. Something occurred to me. A thought I had never bothered entertaining before.

We were less than pets.

We were less than animals who did nothing more than feed off the generosity of the masters. I had killed for mine. I had endured countless perversities in the minds of both men and women for the benefit of the man who owned me. I thought about the name I had once had as a child. Xzya. Why had we ceased to use it? Perhaps I had once been something more than...more than this person-who-was-not-a-person I was now. I fought to pull the memory forward in my mind...

"Today is your birthday, did you know that?"

"Yes."

"I have a special gift for you. Tell me your name."

"Xzya."

"Not anymore. From now on, you have no name."

"Why not?"

"You aren't safe with a name. I'm keeping you safe from people who might hurt you. Do you understand? Good. That's a good girl."

Before I could finish chasing the threads of an almost forgotten birthday through my memories, my door buzzed open at last. I stared at it for a second, debating whether ignoring the implied summons would be worth the reprimand. In the end, I got to my feet.

This time, the only door in the corridor that had been left open for me led to the sitting room where Xzan and his wife usually entertained guests. It was only mildly more comfortable than Xzan's office. While it still boasted the shiny metallic walls that made up every building in Atlantis, this room did have a plush sofa with some lounge chairs set up in a circle. Thick red curtains, meant to block out the suns during the days when they never set, hung from the windows. The curtains were a luxury, though; every home had shutters on the exterior of the buildings which would automatically close at a set time to mimic the night. Some families even programmed the shutters to display a holographic image of the broken moon with its stars.

My master, who could afford fucking curtains, thought such things as stars were unnecessary.

His wife had asked once.

"But Xzan darling, the Norrell's even programmed theirs to look out over the ocean," she crooned while staring at the closed shutters. I had stood a little straighter, for the first time hoping the wife might sway her husband.

"My dear, the Norrell's shave the heads of their slaves and paint them silver. Shall we follow them in that lunacy too?"

I suppose his comment was why she glanced in my direction a moment later. She saw the way I had perked up, my whole body sitting at attention while I waited to hear if my dream to see the stars, even holographic ones, might come true.

She quickly waved her hand with a feigned disinterest in her own request. "You're right, of course. We have gone without it this long, why waste the credits?"

Avah Collier was such a tiny woman for so much disdain to reside in, yet when I walked into the room, I could feel it rolling off of her in waves. She was absolutely lost in the layers of her clothes. Among the monotonous tones of the sitting room, I knew her only by the burst of colour clashing with the curtains next to her. She wore a satin sapphire turban to match the rest of her garments, and to hide thin white hair which had once been a brilliant golden mane. Dainty beaded slippers peaked out of the bottom of her azure skirts, glittering as brightly as the many rings on her fingers. The sheer veil she would wear out in public was hanging limply from one side of her head. She acknowledged my entrance by turning her head as far as she could to avoid any accidental glance in my direction. There was a time I might have returned the sentiment by glaring back at her, but with maturity came the realization I was better off invisible to a woman like Avah Collier.

She stood by the largest window in the room, staring down into the streets of the city. Her eyes examined each of the passing vehicles as though she could distinguish the passengers from twenty floors up. It was nearly noon, yet the lingering night had not yet begun to hint at an anticipated sunrise in the distance. The lights in the room were made brighter by the glare of solar lights meant to mimic the effects of the sun on our moods and body chemistry. Xzan sat at ease on one corner of his couch. He was dressed less ostentatiously than his wife, keeping to the same black robe, leggings, and boots as the day before. When I glanced towards his hands, he gestured to a cushion on the floor. I knelt, settling myself so I was resting my backside on the heels of my own bare feet. Xzan let one hand fall to the back of my neck, kneading my flesh absently while the other hand drummed inpatient fingers against his thigh.

Thomas was not in sight. The only other slaves were the ones coming and going to refill the master's drinks. A tray of ENSA cubes the size of peas created a beautiful tower on the short table before me. It remained untouched. When I finally realized what they were all waiting for, it was because the prodigal son himself was already bursting through the door.

Lark Collier shed his hooded, wine-coloured robe the moment he was through the door, letting it fall to the floor, where it settled like a pool of coagulated blood. Beneath it, he was dressed not unlike his father: all in black except for a dark red sash tied in layers around his waist. Although usually slicked back, his dark hair was overgrown and hung listlessly off his face when he swung his head in annoyance. Dungeon had left new circles under his eyes, aging him more than it would on someone else whose face was not already made up of too many sharp angles. There was a grim set to his pouty lips that hadn't been there before either. The trial had not been kind to him, and as one privy to the darker pleasures of men, I could only guess what might have happened to him in Dungeon. The smile he offered his mother did nothing to hide the effects of the past weeks; it merely served to animate an emaciated corpse.

Mrs. Collier squealed with delight at the sight of her son, throwing herself into Lark's arms before he could even cross the room.

"Oh, my sweet boy! Are you alright?" she pulled back from the embrace to examine his face, turning it side to side to properly assess his condition. There was a fading bruise on one cheek, but I imagined whoever gave him that was now dead. Xzan had as many allies in prison as out. "I am so glad you are home where you belong."

"No thanks to that crooked lawyer," Lark sneered, turning to glare at his father who had remained seated. "Where did you dig up a hack like that?"

Xzan's voice scraped over his son and his hand on my neck squeezed painfully. "Mandar is the best in the city. The fact he couldn't bribe you out of a guilty verdict has a lot more to do with your actual guilt than his incompetence. I thought we discussed the difference between play-things and women of substance."

Lark made a face before plunking himself into the chair across from us. When his eyes travelled hungrily over my body, I pretended not to notice. Too bad a week surrounded by brutish men hadn't altered his taste for female flesh. I settled my mind into the comfortable cocoon of safety that came from knowing that if there was one thing Xzan did not permit, it was his son laying so much as a finger on me. His treatment of the other slave women was well known and had resulted in quick body disposals on more than one occasion. Still, I could never quite feel at ease when those empty eyes were on me. My skin crawled even when I pointedly looked the other way.

Finally, I felt his gaze slide away. I looked up to see him smirking at his father. "The bitch deserved it. It's not like the baby was even mine – she told me so herself – she just wanted my fortune."

"You mean *my* fortune," Xzan scoffed.

Lark waved a dismissive hand through the air.

"And the infant? And the four other men and women in the room?" Xzan laughed but his fingers digging into my flesh belied his anger. I struggled not to whimper. "You acted rash, Lark, and you made us all look foolish in your wake. I am trying to run a business, to build an empire, and you are working incredibly hard to run it into the ground."

Lark held up a glass of amber liquid he had managed to acquire from a passing slave. "Take the legal fees out of my allowance."

"Oh, really, that isn't unnecessary," Mrs. Collier insisted, shooting her husband a venomous glare while settling herself next to their son. She took his hands in hers again, only to have him pull them free. "Your father is just upset over this whole unfortunate incident. But you are home now. We can put it all behind us."

There were several minutes where the only sound was Mrs. Collier nattering on about what social events Lark had missed and the dinner they would be attending a few nights hence. I tuned them out, indulging the heaviness of my eyes until I could almost feel a single sun on my face and the soft scratch of grass on my legs. Xzan rising from the couch brought me crashing back to reality. Reality seemed a dismal place by comparison. Mrs. Collier was leaving to prepare for having drinks with friends. Now I would be alone with the two most dangerous men in Atlantis. One because of the power he could wield over my fate, the other simply because I was sure he was a psychopath with eyes that pierced my soul.

"Still pampering the special one, I see," Lark quipped, pouring himself another drink from a carafe left on the table. I managed to only glare at his boots. "I think she's getting a little insolent if you ask me. It wouldn't hurt to use the rod on occasion."

A gentle hand stroked the side of my face. I leaned into it, provoking Lark by raising my eyes to meet his. He had the cold grey stare of his mother, and it drove the temperature of the room down when he recognized my defiance. "Sometimes, the greatest loyalty is one born from love. I raised this one from an infant. I am the only master she has known or will ever know. One day, perhaps you will understand the difference between fear and reverence. She knows her place better than you know yours."

"You are a blind fool if you think this one lacks teeth. She's just another pretty face among hundreds of others."

"She is more than that," Xzan sighed, beckoning me to stand with him. He turned to face me, lifting my chin with a curved finger. "Go back to your room. Be ready to leave in an hour. I'll give you instructions before you go."

I nodded, brushing past Lark as if he were not blocking my path to the door with his purposefully extended elbow. The younger Collier inhaled deeply as I passed. When the door closed behind me, I was shaking. Lark was mean and more than a little dangerous. While it used to ease the tediousness of life to provoke him, the game was becoming decidedly more perilous now that I was dealing with a man instead of a boy. I consoled myself by imagining I could get him alone in my white room. In the Dream, no man could take ownership of me while in my little white room.

I was startled to find Thomas leaning against the wall next to my door. He stood straighter when he saw me approach, his face expressionless. "I was told to guard your door. Xzan said to use only enough force to restrain and not kill."

There was a question somewhere in there, but I was too tired to puzzle it out. "Have fun with that."

I moved to walk past him; he reached out to stop me. "Who am I watching for in the master's own house?"

There it was. The real question. I smiled wearily. "Haven't you heard? The master's son is home."

Chapter 7

There was little to do to pass the time, and there was only so many times I could check my appearance in the mirror. I stretched. I paced. I tried to get some sleep. I had had my books taken by Mrs. Collier more than a week ago. She hadn't taken Lark's sentencing very well, and she needed to take her frustration out on someone. After storming around the apartment for days, she'd shown up in my room. Her eyes took in my little cubicle with what I thought might be pity, until she saw the book open in my lap as well as the two others I kept propped up on my bed stand.

"Where did you get these?" she snarled as she snatched all three precious items from me.

"The master gave them to me," I told her toes.

Avah seemed unable to speak. I could hear the click of her teeth as she chewed on all the angry words she wanted to say. "You're a liar," she said at last. "These are invaluable, and they are wasted on an illiterate wretch like you."

She left then, though I could not be sure she did not see the angry tears that escaped down my cheeks. I had few enough treasures without her spite to take them all away.

Her assumptions regarding my literacy skills were misplaced of course. Many slaves could read, though not always as well as the masters. It was a game for us. Before I was taken into this life of solitude I inhabited now, my grandmother had taught me alongside several other slave children. We argued over the letters she wrote, swelling with pride every time she smiled at our successes. Even when we got a word wrong, she smiled. Sometimes I think she always smiled, although it could just be a trick of wishful memories.

As for the books, Xzan had given them to me on my birthday the year before. I swear he only remembered the day because it marked the anniversary of the acquisition of his secret weapon, making his gift as much about his own pride than it was about me. I hadn't allowed myself to feed the resentment. I appreciated the books too much. The smell of the musty old pages and the way the ancient paper crinkled between my fingers, reminded me I was part of a world beyond clean, metallic lines.

Cranky old bitch better not have ruined them, I grumbled to myself when I remembered how happy I had been to call them my own. Normally birthdays were hardly worth remembering. They forced me to remember turning five, when Xzan had taken my name away, as if the absence of a name was a present in itself. That was also the day my grandmother died. Birthdays are overrated.

In any event, it was with pure relief that I bounded down the hall towards Xzan's office when my buzzer sounded an hour later. Thomas was already there, being lectured by Xzan about the procedures to come. Thomas was kneeling, appropriately submissive. He did not so much as glance my direction when I silently knelt beside him for the rest of the lecture.

"You will remain outside the door the entire time. No one is to interrupt her, do you understand?" Thomas nodded, his mouth a thin line. "Good. You will have more trouble than the last guard because of your station. Keep this on you in case any physical altercation results in the authorities being called. It will grant you immunity from judgement until I have had a chance to speak in your defense."

Thomas accepted the small comm disc – when activated, Xzan's likeness would appear to announce the bearer's purpose and connections – that was offered, his eyes never leaving a singular spot on the floor. Even when he stood to leave, it seemed as though the spot was leading the way, so fearsome was his concentration on something we couldn't see. I watched his retreating heels until Xzan bid me to stand to hear my task. Only then was I permitted to look up at my master.

"I want you to find out what the Public Trade Act is, when it will be implemented, and the names of anyone who can stop it from happening. Do you understand?"

"Yes."

"Good," Xzan smiled. It left little crinkles around his eyes, the only evidence of his age, though it did nothing to warm them. "I'm worried the recent decline in tradable goods is giving certain people grand ideas. I would hate to be the one who has to watch them fail."

He hooked an arm around my waist to guide me towards the door. Before he sent me through, he paused. "Let's try not to kill anyone tonight, alright?" His eyes were specifically on Thomas. Indulging my own slight smile, I bowed my head and left.

We took the slave elevator down to the main floor, neither one of us talking to the other. I wondered at the absence of Thomas' earlier friendliness, missed it even, until I decided he was simply taking my warning about the cameras and Xzan's rules seriously. It was about time. I certainly didn't care to find myself on the receiving end of a lash just because he was trained in a pit of savages. Still, I found myself glancing over at him more than I bothered watching where I stepped. When my heel snagged a seam in the paneled floors, my inattention pitched me forward toward the glass doors of the building's entrance. A strong hand caught me by the arm, pulling me back to a position of balance. Though I felt his grip after he let go, it hadn't lingered a moment longer than was necessary for me to catch my balance.

Our silence lasted all the way until we found our seats in the back of the family car. The partition was down so the driver-program could record us speaking if we chose to. For a while we decided not to say anything, but soon the frosty sensation coming from the man next to me was too much to bear.

"Thanks for catching me back there," I tried. Gratitude seemed a safe enough topic, even if we were being watched.

Thomas stared out into the night.

"You know, Hal wasn't much of a conversationalist either, but at least he looked at the person he was supposed to be babysitting every so often," I muttered, intentionally loud enough to be heard.

A grunt. That was the extent of his reply.

Losing all interest in the person in the driver's seat, whose holographic ears actually seemed to be growing larger, I turned to execute the full measure of my glare on the man next to me. By rights he should have burst into flames. Instead, he met my fury with a wall of ice.

"So, this is it?" Thomas asked at last.

"Excuse me?"

"I almost hoped you were just a favourite pet, maybe even his favourite bastard, but this?" he shook his head. "You don't even fight it. You just let your body be used for the whims of an old man and his friends."

He must have expected a reply, an angry denial or righteous justification of my role in this world, but when he turned his face back to me the sound of my palm crossing Thomas' cheek made the driver glitch in his seat.

"How dare you judge me!" I spat. "You know nothing of my place in this world, in this terrible, corrupt city. There *is* nothing else. Only the life we are given to live. I do what I do because the alternative is death."

"That is no life."

"You have no idea what you're talking about." I turned away from him to hide the burning in my cheeks. "I've never even..." I stopped, not sure where to go with my train of thought. I didn't owe this stranger an explanation, so why did I feel my stomach twisting on the words I had to swallow. "I have no choice," I finished lamely.

If anything, the temperature in the vehicle dipped further. "I would die before I let myself be used as you are being used."

I turned to smile sadly at him. "If that were true, you'd already be dead, Mr. Undefeated-Champion. We're all being used for something, whether it's heating the blood or spilling it. It's all the same thing in the end." I left Thomas to ponder my words and heard nothing more from him the rest of the drive.

Thomas

Thomas could hardly stand the pain of opening his eyes. Sand and other grit tore at the inside of his lids, but he was too cold to sleep any longer. He had made it to the top of the beanstalk, glanced up at the stars in this strange new world, then promptly fell asleep. Now it was time to explore where he had ended up, but every muscle in his body protested the slightest movement. It had seemed to take days to ascend the beanstalk, though for a long time Thomas only traveled through a land of night so he couldn't be sure. He had climbed through the heavens themselves, admired stars shooting past his perch, and wondered if there were other worlds thriving and failing in the sparkling lights off in the distance. The magic in the air tasted sweet on his tongue and he would have stayed in that space forever if a little voice in his head hadn't urged him forward.

His adventure was still waiting.

Now that he had arrived wherever it was the magic had sent him, he couldn't help his disappointment at the barren land around him. The heat bore down on him, even where he was still sheltered by a single broad leaf from his beanstalk. The leaf was all that was left of the behemoth that had sprung from three tiny beans, and it was shriveling into the same putrid brown as the earth outside its shadows. Thomas strained to see some sign of life beyond the hard-packed dirt and shifting dunes surrounding him. There was something wrong with the sky, too. It was less a vibrant blue than the filthy hue of a storm cloud. Looking around once more, Thomas assured himself there were no immediate signs of danger. He crawled cautiously out from his shriveling shelter. Judging by the rough sand beneath him, he imagined this land hadn't seen a storm cloud in a long time.

As soon as he was free of its shadow, the leaf curled up into itself before crumbling into a pile of shredded rubbish. Thomas squared his shoulders beneath his sweat drenched shirt. "I'm here for an adventure," he reminded himself.

He raised his chin to find the sun, certain at least his sense of direction would remain the same in this strange land. Whether the sun set in the east or the west, the north or the south, it would at least give him a steady source of guidance. Except, to his wonder and dismay, there were two suns scorching the earth from their lofty heights. One glowed much as Thomas remembered his own sun: white-hot and bright over the far horizon to his right. Had it been the sun he'd always known, its position might have suggested mid-afternoon. The second sun was darker, a golden orange eye that glared at him from directly overhead. Thomas shook his head twice and rubbed his eyes in a futile attempt to banish at least one of the fiery orbs from the sky.

Taking comfort in the familiarity of the larger sun already beginning its descent, Thomas decided to follow its path across the sky. He started walking.

After several hours he stopped. Neither sun seemed to have moved. His feet sloshed in puddles of their own making inside his boots, and when he raised a hand to shade his squinting eyes, the skin crinkling on his face cracked and began to weep. Something didn't feel right about the eerie stillness of the suns. He swallowed past his swollen tongue and kept moving.

When he fell to his knees before a blackened, dead bush, Thomas no longer knew how much time had come to pass. The larger sun had finally begun to move, he was sure of it. It rested a hand's-width above the horizon, though its brother had scarcely moved at all. Thomas' lips were broken, his eyes half-blinded by the glare of light off the unforgiving landscape. He thought he would die. When the bush quivered and spoke, Thomas thought his god had come to forgive him for the hubris of his ill-conceived adventure. He closed his eyes and he fell on his face, giving in to merciful darkness.

When he woke again, he wanted to weep. Had he been forsaken? The heat rising from the ground could only be the fires of Hell consuming his soul.

"I think it's awake."

Thomas jerked his head toward where the blackened bush was speaking to a comrade. "Sure looks that way." Came the reply. "You better pay up, Shael. I told ya we'd find a Wilder before we got home."

"A half dead whelp is hardly a Wilder," Shael pouted before approaching where Thomas still lay on the ground. The closer the talking bush moved, the more it materialized into a robed figure, a man, whose pale eyes almost glowed out of his tanned face. "Hardly worth the water you dumped down its throat."

"It'll make a good fighter, I bet," the companion spoke again, pulling back his hood to wipe his brow with his sleeve. "Anything that can survive out here is a born fighter."

Thomas was yanked to his knees by his hair by a grinning Shael. "I don't know, Alder. Once we soften up the skin on its lips it might do well serving in the pleasure houses. It has a pretty mouth, after all. They'll pay extra for those exotic eyes too."

Thomas' heart beat faster. Though their words stuck in the back of their throats when they spoke, their English as he knew it was clear enough. Anger swelled in Thomas' chest. He worked up enough saliva to spit at Shael's feet before pressing his swollen lips together.

"What'd I tell ya? A fighter."

Shael's eyes had darkened, and he was fiddling with whatever held the many layers of his robe together. Thomas refused to look at the pale appendage he had exposed. "Damn Wilder needs to be shown his place."

In the moment it took Shael to yank Thomas' head forward, Thomas had decided he would rather die than give in to such humiliation. His teeth locked down with every ounce of strength he still had, and he waited for the blow that would put him out of his misery. When it came, it only filled his head with stars. Thomas spat blood onto the ground and rolled away from where Shael was dancing in pain, screeching like a crazed cat. Alder recovered from his laughter enough to stand and approach his struggling companion.

"Shut up, you fool!" he commanded with casual annoyance. He reached up to grab his friend's blubbering face in his hands. "You deserved that and you know it." In one swift movement, Shael's head was jerked to the side with a sharp crack.

Thomas looked up at Alder with a challenge in his eyes. "I will not serve at anyone's pleasure." He resisted the urge to wipe the blood from his chin.

"Oh, my friend, you will serve and, even better, you will make me as rich as a Collier," Alder was smiling. He took the water bag from Shael's corpse and threw it at Thomas. "You will fight for me when we get back to Atlantis. You will fight, and I will make sure you live long enough to get there."

When they started off again, Thomas wondered at the land he had come to. Perhaps he had not escaped his fate at all. Perhaps his fate had *only changed its clothes, still stringing him along at the other end of a thick chain as they continued their trek through the desert.*

Time continued to slog along no matter how far they walked. Even Alder was beginning to falter. Thomas could not figure out how the man managed beneath all those robes, the heat was oppressive enough without the weight of extra clothes. Then again, Thomas knew if he survived long enough to find shelter, his exposed skin would be sore for weeks before it finally started to peel.

"There it is, Wilder," Alder said at last. He came to a stop long enough to take a long drink from his water bottle and allow Thomas the same luxury.

Thomas looked to where Alder was gesturing with an outstretched hand. At first, he could see nothing but a hazy smudge against the horizon. It was only after they began walking again did Thomas realize he was staring at the greatest wall he had ever seen. It stretched on forever in both directions. As they approached its shadow, Thomas could only just make out the bobbing heads of men stalking along the top. It was not made of any stone Thomas had ever encountered either. Its smooth surface glimmered in the light of the suns, and the air around it sent off little waves of heat that toyed with his eyes as he gazed upon it.

Alder seemed to enjoy Thomas' awe. The gate they passed through was made of the same shiny material. Thomas watched in amazement as Alder pushed a button on the wall next to it, and the image of a man in miniature appeared before them.

"Alder Barracks returning with one slave for the pits," Alder declared.

The little man shivered as he moved to look both the slaver and the slave up and down. "You registered to leave with Shael Yodanna as well. Where is he?"

"Fell in a crevice and died," Alder replied simply. He didn't even bother to sound regretful at the loss of his companion.

The little man winked out of existence as quickly as he had appeared. Then the gate slid up into the wall to allow them through. Thomas clicked his mouth shut in amazement. Alder chuckled at the way the boy seemed determined to hide his amazement.

"You haven't seen anything yet, little Wilder," Alder promised. As they lost themselves in a maze of strange vehicles and glittering buildings,

the slaver's voice reached Thomas' ears over the din of the city. "Welcome to Atlantis."

Chapter 8

Thomas' words bothered me more than they should have. The very thought of what he assumed I was doing made my skin scrawl. *Fucking bastard*, I cursed him. What right did he have to judge me, as if I truly did the things those men and women fantasized about? It wasn't real. None of it was. Everything that happened in the Dream was nothing but...but what?

My lips turned down at the corners, pulling my mood down with them.

If the Dream was mine, did I really need the rest of it to accomplish what I set out to do? In the Dream I was the Master. I could make those I brought with me do whatever I pleased. So, why did I let them take their pleasure with me?

As the streetlights of Atlantis passed by our car, one by one by one, I began to go over all the people Xzan had set me on. Their faces flashed in front of my eyes, one by one by one, and with each memory I squirmed under the weight of the images of what we had done in the Dream. It was like watching a movie in reverse, all the way back to the beginning, to the very first target Xzan had given me.

I was sixteen at the time, already well on my way to the full blossom of womanhood. Xzan had called me to his office, but when I got there, he wasn't alone.

The stranger's name was Dinah. From the first moment I made the mistake of glancing up at him, I felt a shiver of trepidation ripple across my body. Xzan crossed the room to where I found myself frozen by the entrance. His hands on my shoulders felt heavy and almost reassuring.

"It's time," he spoke so softly I almost missed his words with the heavy beat of my heart in my ears. "It is just like we practiced. I want you to use your gift and find out which mayoral candidate he's backing. Then, you'll put him down. Do you understand?"

His fingers grabbed my jaw then so hard I had no choice but to look up at him. He repeated the question.

"Do you understand me?"

"Yes, master," I breathed.

"Good," Xzan fixed a smile on his face before he turned back to his guest.

"She is a beauty," Dinah said with the subtle undertones of a conversation picking up where it left off. "I still think it's terribly rude of you to bring her out just to rub my face in your good fortune. That is, unless you lied when you said she wasn't for sale."

Xzan laughed. "No. I will never part with this one," he replied, guiding me further into the room with a hand at the small of my back. "She promises to bring me great pleasure someday."

Dinah raised one dark eyebrow. "You mean, you haven't tried her out yet?"

"Of course not," Xzan's annoyance sounded genuine, and his hand twitched against my back. "She's hardly more than a child."

"If you say so." I could feel Dinah's disagreement in the way his eyes slid over my body. I was trembling.

"You know, I think I left that paperwork you were after in the sitting room," Xzan spoke up suddenly. "I'll go get it so we can finish our business and find something more enjoyable to do."

Xzan left me in the company of a predator. I had no idea what to do next. I knew how to get to the Dream, how to bend it to my will, but I had never taken another person with me before. My grandmother had taught me how to see the window in their eyes, but so far, I had learned everything Xzan told me to do by pure instinct.

"Don't be frightened," Dinah spoke up as he moved towards where I stood in the middle of the room. "You can look up at me if you want. I'm a little more modern than some of the other masters."

I held my breath as I raised my eyes to his. They were blue, though his dilated pupils nearly wiped the colour out completely, and he was standing closer to me than I'd thought. I could smell the sweat beading around the edge of his emerald turban.

With his invitation to look, I examined his intense stare, looking for my window to the Dream. I thought I could see it, a sliver of light in the darkness, but my heart was racing and fear was turning my knees to jelly. When Dinah brought his hand up near my face, I gasped at the unexpected sensation of his skin against mine. No one had touched me in years. At least, no one other than Xzan, who sometimes offered a patient pat on the head. At the sight of my unease, the sliver became an open door, and in a state of sheer panic, I plunged us both towards the Dream.

That first time with another person was terrifying. I had no idea where I was, or even if I had managed to bring Dinah with me. The world blurred and slurred together in a swirl of colour while it fought for some semblance of reality. I could feel my body falling away from me and I thought I might float away completely. I wondered if it would be so bad if I never returned to the suit of flesh that anchored me in a world with invisible chains.

Dinah's Dream was unique. I had never seen one quite like it before, and I have never encountered one like it since. The world around us shimmered with colour that never quite settled on any perceivable hue. I could feel the solidity of the floor beneath my feet, yet I couldn't see it beyond the haze of fluttering air. All I could see was Dinah, standing uncomfortably close to me. We were encased in silence, or at least, I was. I watched Dinah smile. I watched the smooth movement of soft lips as he spoke. No sounds reached my ears. This unnerved me more than anything. I wanted to know what he was saying – needed to know – so I focused every thought in my mind on defeating the silence.

"...is where I want you."

Once audible, his voice echoed off the inside of my skull and I felt my stomach tighten as a hand grasped my arm. "No," I shouted.

Dinah's face lit up with surprise, but his grip on my arm was tighter than ever. "What do you mean, no?" His voice was not angry. If anything, it was only mildly amused.

"I don't want you to touch me," I managed to whisper, my eyes never rising past the point of his nose. "Please."

"I do like it when you say please," Dinah murmured before he pulled me a bit closer.

My heart raced a little faster and the air around us both shimmered and began to lose its luminescence. I wanted to escape the Dream more than anything in the world. His grip on my arm was like a vice, like the cuffs the doctor used to hold me down when the new growth of hair under my arms needed to be removed with a laser. I began to imagine how scared I was then too, my body held down against the cool steel table, and I felt the world around me begin to shift.

My fear was becoming something else, something more than fear but not quite anger.

I blinked and the tables had turned. I was standing at the edge of a long metal table, staring at Dinah where he was pinned down in a slave's simple white kilt. He fought against the metal cuffs that rose out of the table to encase each bicep. His mouth moved without sound again, but when I finally found my voice, I realized with some satisfaction that he was the only one trapped in silence.

"I said no," I told him, new strength seeping into each word as I spoke. "I am not yours."

Dinah shook his head, his face turning a brilliant shade of red. I touched his cheek, surprised by how warm the flesh felt and fascinated by the stubble I thought I could feel beneath my sensitive fingertips.

"Did you know that all slaves have their hair removed from their bodies?" I asked him. My fingers travelled down to his chest and the few fine hairs growing there. "Why do the Masters get to keep their hair if they choose but not us? I don't understand."

My control must have been slipping, for Dinah managed to choke out a few choice words. "I will kill you."

I shook my head at his promise. Something was changing inside of me, something that would come to replace the terror I had felt earlier. No threats from the vulnerable man before me would ever affect me again. I promised myself that then and there. "No," I told him. "I will kill *you* if you ever touch me again."

Dinah's eyes bulged. Words he thought to spit at me became a gag in his own throat, making it difficult to breathe. While I was fascinated by the way his face began to change from red to purple, I remembered I had a job to do.

"I want you to tell me about the mayor's office..."

With a little more creativity on my part, Dinah told me everything I wanted to know and more. Xzan had been pleased with me that day, and I had basked in his pleasure.

As my thoughts returned to the present, I wondered if I did not find at least some pleasure in what I did. I was a grown woman now. I had already come to realize my Master's pleasure no longer motivated me in the way it used to. I thought about the pleasures my targets often sought from me, and I thought about all the times I had enjoyed it. The problem was, that was often in the moments I gave them control of the Dream. When I took my power back, it was to subjugate them or pull their secrets from their minds. How could I know what was genuine enjoyment on my part, and what was really just a product of their own fantasies?

A shiver passed along my skin, raising the flesh in tingling little bumps.

Thomas' angry words sat even less comfortably than they had before. I wondered if his opinion of me would lessen further if he knew the truth: that I enjoyed my role in bringing the masters to their knees.

Would he be as ashamed of me as I was?

Chapter 9

When we reached the apartment building where my target lived, Thomas held the door for me. Perhaps he meant it as an apology, but I ignored the gesture if only to hold onto my anger a little longer; it would make me sharper when I needed it later. I was familiar with the place we had come to. The man I was to see was Jhondu Sil, the Trade Minister's assistant. He was a nobody in the grand scheme of things, but he was privy to many things that went on in the Mayor's office that others would not know. He came from a powerful family, one that would see him mayor someday if he played his cards right, so he rarely ever questioned Xzan's seeming generosity when I came to visit. It was only his due after all.

The doorman was expecting us. He took us to the slave's elevator and programmed our stop without one word passing his lips. Thomas opened his mouth to speak. I studiously ignored the effort. When we stepped off the lift, we were in the laundry room of Jhondu's home and a sudden inconvenience to two women working there. One almost dropped her basket of neatly folded sheets at the sight of Thomas, his head all but brushing the low ceiling. The second woman tried to hide her admiration of his exotic presence in an air of authority, showing us the way to the sitting room where Jhondu was entertaining guests.

Xzan had forgotten to mention this, of course. Group situations were dangerous. I had never tried to deal with more than one Dreamer at a time. I wasn't sure it was even possible. The dozen or so other people would overpower any resistance from Thomas no matter how big and intimidating he made himself. Luckily for me, Jhondu was nearly done with his company.

"Looks like the bribe has arrived," he laughed when he beckoned me across the room. "Xzan always sends this little prize when he wants something."

"As if she's that good," someone snickered behind a glass of spirits. He was rewarded for his comment with a round of laughter at my expense.

"I assure you my friend, she's that good," Jhondu told the speaker, pulling me down to sit on his knee once I was close enough to get a hold of. "Spend a night with her and you're likely to forget your name by morning."

Another wave of rustling laughter. I imagined doing that very thing to Jhondu; making him forget his name. I imagined making all of them as nameless as a slave. *Would they still be laughing then?* It was a welcome distraction while I endured the gawking and the groping of his friends, as well as the return of Thomas' judgement rippling through the air from the doorway. Eventually, the other men and women returned to the conversation they had left off when I arrived.

"Why aren't they more worried about the fissure? Surely they can't ignore the fact that these quakes are becoming more frequent."

My eyes trailed along the carpeted floor to rest on the knees of the woman who I thought had spoken. I stayed focused on the gold embroidery of her robe to hide my interest in the conversation they were eager to resume.

"They aren't that frequent," a man's voice interjected. "One quake every year or two isn't exactly uncommon."

"Never as strong as that last one," the woman replied. Her voice held more than a hint of panic and I watched as she uncrossed her legs only to cross them again the other way. "Maybe you can't feel them up on the top floor of your building, but I promise you the instruments in the lab tell us it was stronger than anything we've ever felt before. Even the scouts on the wall claim they saw the sea waters rise as if to consume us. If our ancestors hadn't built it so high..." her voice trailed off.

Jhondu shifted beneath me. "The fissure is of no threat to us." One hand left my leg to bring his drink to his lips. "If anything, it will swallow any Wilders still left in the world and leave Atlantis safe behind her wall. Good riddance to any poor soul outside our city."

"Then where will I get a good fighter?"

A muffled round of laughter floated around us.

"But seriously," Jhondu went on. "Our buildings are built to withstand a shudder or two. The last time I even noticed a quake was over ten years ago. The world may someday crumble away, the sea draining with it, but Atlantis will remain forever." His confidence was such there was no doubt remaining in the murmured agreement or clink of glasses toasting the greatness of our city.

I sat there wondering what a fissure was and if it truly could swallow the city. I lost myself in the fantasy for a time. In my mind, a great hole opened under my feet, welcoming me into a dark embrace. I imagined death to be a dreamless sleep, and the thought was somehow comforting.

In the real world I tried to speed things along, especially when the weight of my eyelids made alertness difficult to maintain. I shifted just enough to raise Jhondu's awareness of his proximity to my body. A little shuffle this way then that created some gentle friction, enough to get the after-party started. At last, Jhondu stood to bid his guests farewell, one arm still holding me before him to hide his rather obvious anticipation. One by one, he said good-bye to each companion until it was only the three of us left in the room.

"Does he always look so serious?" Jhondu asked good-naturedly, standing right under Thomas' nose to examine him. "You know, I think I bet on you in the pits once. Won a few credits if I remember correctly."

"He is not permitted to watch," I said huskily, slipping my arm around Jhondu's waist to distract him. It worked.

"It's a shame, big fellow," Jhondu gave Thomas a pat on the shoulder. "We'll be worth watching."

I kept my smile plastered to my face all the way to the bedroom. Only when the door slid closed did it falter. I had been with Jhondu before, but this time felt different. I tried to not to tell myself it was because Thomas was outside the door, thoroughly pissed off and thinking the worst of me. No, that wasn't at all distracting.

I used my annoyance as a focus point to concentrate on while I primed Jhondu for the Dream. With him, there was no need for promises. He didn't drink or smoke, the usual ways to make someone malleable without offering sex; he was an open-minded kind of person by nature. His honesty was like having a door opened to me at all times. I didn't even need to take him all the way to the Dream. While my own distraction slowed the process, I managed to get him to the dream-like trance I preferred for interrogations without even touching him. After only a few moments of his eyes following the sway of my hips while I hummed an old song, I used my hands against my body to draw his eyes up to mine. That was all it took, really. He sat in a chair staring off into space while I sat on the edge of the bed maintaining eye contact so I could tell if the trance wavered.

"What is the Public Trade Act?" I asked pointedly, anxious to be done with this.

"It will grant the Mayor and his council the right to sell slaves at a fair public market instead of the private auctions."

"Why is this so important?"

Jhondu shrugged. "Too few people are benefiting from the most profitable trade in Atlantis. Why should the Colliers of the world reap all the rewards? We pride ourselves on how far we've come since the near extinction of our ancestors. Our city is strong and the famines are over. We should clean up the drudgery still out on the streets and make sure there is a slave for every hard-working family in Atlantis as a reward for their efforts. Profits can support social programs and allow all civilians to thrive. Private sales will be heavily taxed to add to Atlantis' coffers."

He spoke like he was making a campaign promise. *He must write the Mayor's speeches too.* I grimaced. "When is the vote?"

"The council votes on it at the first meeting after the mayor is re-sworn in this week."

"Will it pass?"

Jhondu leaned forward in his chair, almost making me lose control of the link as a measure of his eagerness stirred within his unseeing eyes. "Oh, yes. All the council members are on board and the mayor has no desire to squash it. We stand to generate a great deal of influence here."

Credits. He must mean credits; if Xzan had taught me anything, it was that all power came from the control of wealth. Wealth controlled people. Xzan was the largest contributor of campaign funds in every election, and the candidate with his support always won. Without the financing he offered, there would be no government, not even the current illusion of one where the Colliers pulled most of the strings. While I weaved a dream for Jhondu to sleep on, I wanted to laugh at the mayor's feeble attempt at betrayal. Even without me to spy on them, this plan would never work. *Would it?*

I hesitated in my task. What if Xzan was no longer the most powerful man in the city? What would that mean for me? Would he still find me useful, or would he find a new use for me altogether? Could Xzan destroy the Council in time to save his own bottom line if the law had already been passed? Before I could snap out of my own thoughts, something snapped around my wrist.

"Where are you going?" Jhondu's eyes were still somewhat clouded, the window to the Dream wide open though I had pulled my influence from it.

"I'm not going anywhere," I purred, trying to settle him back against his chair so I could re-establish my control.

"I'm not nearly finished with you yet." Jhondu pressed forward so suddenly I stumbled and broke eye contact. By the time I regained my mental footing, his mouth was on mine, his eyes were firmly shut, and he was pushing me back towards the bed. Try as I might, I couldn't push him off; his guard was down, yet there was nothing I could do about it. His eyelids were as impenetrable as a solid wall. The back of my knees caught the edge of the bed. As I fell, I felt the first swell of panic in my chest.

"Hey, slow down," I tried to keep the sultry in my tone. I tried to weave my fingers into his hair to pull back his head. "I want you to look at me."

He growled into my shoulder, struggling to free himself from his clothes while still trying to get into mine. *Just look at me!* I wanted to scream.

"Stop, please," I tried, my voice firm but free of demand. I couldn't tell if the man on top of me was the master or the Dreamer. I gave him a mighty shove, my voice rising in pitch and desperation. "Get off of me!"

Jhondu pulled back from my neck, meeting my eyes at last. It was there. I saw it. There was a fantasy playing out just behind his consciousness, only it was happening for real, and Jhondu was merely a sleepwalker at the mercy of his dreams. He was not really there behind those eyes, instead it was the beast I had created with his Dream. Before I could puzzle out how to undo my careless mistake, Jhondu was pulled off me with such force I was obliged to follow him to the floor. Thomas was standing over the master's limp body, fists raised and ready to fall. In a brief moment of clarity, I scrambled between the two of them.

"Stop!" I cried, facing Thomas with my hands raised. "If you hurt him, they will kill you."

Thomas took several steadying breaths, slowly lowering his hand when he noticed the man on the floor was making no effort to get up anyway. "I heard you cry out."

I sat on the ground with a swift grunt of relief. I smoothed my hair off my face to regain some composure, and pretended I didn't notice how badly my hands were shaking. "Yes, well, things definitely weren't going my way."

I wanted to cry and laugh at the same time. Of all the experiences I had had in the Dream, of all the twisted fantasies I had been privy to, the reality of what these men wanted from me was so much more terrifying. Instead of giving in to the conflicting reactions resonating in my mind, I turned to survey the damage. Thomas had not injured Jhondu too badly as far as I could tell. If anything, he had done what I did not: lock him properly in a dream. I found a small lump on the back of Jhondu's head, hidden perfectly by his hair. *Great. Maybe he'll forget his name after all.* The thought passing through my head brought hysterical giggles bubbling back to the surface. I had to hold them in by pressing the back of my hand to my lips.

"Get him on the bed, please," I instructed Thomas, beating him there so I could properly make a mess of the sheets. Not that we hadn't already done some damage. Thomas was silent, even after helping me undress the man who was now moaning as he regained consciousness. "Go wait for me by the door."

I didn't wait to see if Thomas obeyed. Jhondu's eyes were fluttering open, his body twisting in the sheets as if he had forgotten getting tangled up in them. Just as he was starting to mutter and raise his hand to his head, I leaned over him, ready to meet his eyes as soon as they opened. When they did, the Dream was gone but not the opportunity to bring it back.

"That was amazing," I murmured softly, as if our wrestling match had taken my breath away; actually, I suppose it had. Jhondu offered me a sleepy smile as I wound a strand of his hair on my finger. "Care to go again?" Jhondu nodded.

I took myself to the Dream just long enough to fix the fantasy in Jhondu's mind. When I pulled free once more, Jhondu was snoring quietly, his mouth appropriately slack. I didn't dare smile; instead, I allowed myself to feel the bone-deep exhaustion that comes from exerting too much energy for whatever power gave me my gift. Every muscle protested when I stood up. A sigh swept the rest of the tension from my body. My steps toward the door seemed more like the deflated dance of an empty bag on the wind.

"What was that?"

Thomas' presence at the door stopped me in my tracks. I thought he had left the room. Instead, he had witnessed what I was. What had he really seen, though – me staring into the eyes of a man who now slept as any properly sated man should sleep? That was all it could be. Right?

"I tucked him in. That bump on his head knocked him right out," I hedged. If I could have swept by Thomas then, I would have. Unfortunately, that would have been like trying to walk through a wall. He was blocking the door with his body and the lock was still engaged, preventing the door from sliding freely at my approach.

"You did something to him. I saw – " He struggled to put what he saw into words. His hands settled onto my shoulders. "Your eyes. The colour went out of them completely. His, too, just before they closed." He was searching my eyes as if to reassure himself they were the same amber they had always been. "It was like your soul slipped away and all that was left were two empty black pools."

My mouth hung open; I closed it with a snap. No one had described what my gift looked like before. Only Xzan had ever witnessed it, and he had certainly never told me what it was like. I tried to imagine myself as Thomas had seen me: a life-like doll poised in a tableau of seduction. Finally, I said "I made him Dream."

Thomas' head tilted to the right, just enough for a lock of hair to tease the corner of his eye. "Dream?"

"It's what I do," I explained, my thumbs cracking each of my knuckles as I spoke. "I don't do the things you thought – at least, not exactly the way you thought it. I can take the mind of a person to the Dream. I can ask them questions, pass along messages, or even kill them while they remain asleep to the rest of the world. The rest of it, the seduction and teasing, it's just the easiest way to get these men to open their souls to me. I can't take them if they are not somehow vulnerable already."

The whole explanation came out in one breath; at least it felt that way. I was able to take several calm breaths while I waited for Thomas' reaction. I began to squirm under the weight of his hands. "We need to go," I told him, managing not to glance back at the man on the bed. "If he wakes again the false memory of the night will not be strong enough to change what he actually experienced."

Thomas moved out of my way – even unlocking the door for us to pass through – but he remained locked in stoic silence until we were in the car. By then, it was too late to ask questions for fear of being overheard. Instead, startling me enough to make me yelp, Thomas leaned over to whisper in my ear.

"I'm sorry."

I met his eyes, made so much darker by the thin luminescence of the passing streetlamps. I lost myself there for a moment. His barriers were down, open honesty inviting me in to see what hid behind the loneliness and grief. The temptation to make him show me the rest, to drag him into the Dream and explore the Wilder within, made my breath catch in my throat. In the end, all I could manage was a curt nod before my eyes resumed their absent observations of the world passing by outside my window.

I resented the uncertainty his words created inside me.

Chapter 10

Later that night, after explaining what I had uncovered to Xzan, I lay in bed thinking about Thomas. He knew my secret. He knew it and had shown no fear or shock or hatred. Had I really been afraid of that? I didn't think so. The fact that my gift was a secret was to serve Xzan as efficiently as possible. If people knew I could get into their heads, they would probably lock me in Dungeon or cast me into the Wilds instead of risking my influence over them. My secret was for my own protection, I supposed. If someone was able to wrest me away from Xzan, they might find a way to force me to do their bidding instead. Collars such as the one Thomas wore were not as rare as many slaves would like to believe. I would just as soon serve the master I had than risk the untested mercies of another. Yet Thomas has displayed no shock at the brief explanation I had provided him. Perhaps wherever Thomas came from such things were not so rare. Perhaps there were others like me somewhere out in the world; I imagined they used their gifts for something more honourable than espionage and murder. I tried to envision a great land beyond the expanse of the Wilds, where there were Dreamers everywhere and I would be one of many instead of only one. I longed to believe such a land must exist.

When sleep came upon me at last, my dreams took me to a beautiful new world I could never have imagined on my own.

I found myself in an open space outside the city. Only it was not the unrelenting barren Wilds I knew to exist beyond the wall. Instead, I was surrounded by tall green stalks of grass and a myriad of wildflowers that swayed in the wind. I knew I stood in a meadow, for I had read of such things in an old book, but I had never dreamed of one before. My mind should not have been able to recall so many rich details of things I had never experienced or seen in the waking world.

Strange insects with broad white wings fluttered before me like a cloud dancing for my pleasure alone. I laughed and twirled around, raising my hands to the sky as if I might stall them in their flight towards the heavens. As my eyes followed their ascent, I saw flocks of white creatures, their long necks stretched out ahead of them while powerful wings beat against the air, flying overhead in a perfect V-formation. I ran after them, stretching out my arms as if I might join them in the sky.

Their gentle honks called down to me, inviting me to join them, but my feet remained solidly on the earth. I wondered if I could give myself wings and soar with them while in my Dream. It had never occurred to me to fly. Now I fervently wished my arms would become wings to carry me away.

I couldn't believe the blue of the sky; it seemed too perfect to be natural. The vibrance of it enchanted me until I was dizzy from my attempt to see it all at once. I let myself fall back onto the grass, staring at the stalks towering over me. A tiny creature with oddly bent knees clung to one blade, chirping as it rubbed the two strange legs together. Turning my head to one side, I found myself staring into a pair of tiny black eyes. We had rats in Atlantis, so I recognized a rodent when I saw one, but this little ball of fur was much more delicate than the gutter rats of the city. Its whiskers twitched inquisitively before it scurried out of sight.

The wind rustling through the grass joined the chirping insect to sing me a song of peace and tranquility. I thought I heard words whispering within the melody; the lyrics told the tale of valiant men on the backs of proudly prancing beasts. The music spoke of a brave king named Arthur who brought greatness out of his most humble of servants. In the Dream, I closed my eyes to let the story fill my mind. In doing so, I found myself falling into proper sleep. I struggled to decide if the masculine voice singing these stories in my ear was familiar, or simply a fantasy of my own creation.

My usual dreams were more intense than I was used to, even though I was certain they were not another form of the Dream. They were dominated by my grandmother. I could see her standing in complete darkness save for an open door behind her which allowed light to fan out across her person. She didn't speak but her smile filled me with such longing I couldn't help but reach out to her.

Every step I took towards her seemed to move a step back. I started running. My grandmother was swallowed by the light of the doorway, so I followed her. I raised my hands to shield my eyes against the glare.

My grandmother was gone. Instead, I found myself standing in the Wilds. The light was muted somehow, like I was caught in perpetual twilight, though I could see the suns clearly in the sky. The suns were growing steadily as if they meant to collide with the earth. Still the world remained dim. Just as I thought they might hit, all colour snuffed out and I was engulfed in complete darkness.

In the darkness, I thought I saw the subtle glow of stars. Before I could trace the old stories in their growing luminescence, the morning bells tore me from my sleep.

Chapter 11

Thomas was never far from my mind, or my door, for the next several days. It may have been Lark's return, a persistent and ever-present danger to my safety – or even just the lack of necessary overtime pay Hal would have had to receive for such diligence – but Thomas spent every waking moment outside of my door. I suddenly felt like a prisoner, unable to go anywhere without my rather intimidating shadow stalking my every step. Not that I had cause to go anywhere. Xzan seemed to forget my existence for a time. I might have enjoyed it if my door had been opened once or twice, or if it had been thin enough to carry on a conversation with Thomas without raising our voices. I was going slowly insane, trapped in my chambers with only my own company.

I told myself this was life as usual, but my own company was now less desirable than it had been in the past.

Finally, I was called upon to wait on Mrs. Collier and her friends one afternoon. The prospect was unusually welcome after my confinement. This often meant enduring unnecessary conversations about the perverse attraction that their husbands or sons (even daughters, oh my!) had for their servants. Their vapid small talk left me sick to my stomach, but I was anxious to escape the confines of my room even if it was to serve the whims of the entitled. I even took extra care to keep my eyes lowered and my posture properly slouched in deference no matter what insult they murmured in my direction.

For so many generations life had been easy for most Atlantians. The poverty line was almost non-existent, and anyone below it was not considered a member of civilized society. I wondered what we were if not members of society? Certainly not human. The ladies stared down their noses at me and one tripped me with a subtly exposed slippered-foot when I first entered the room. I was a nuisance, and for all I could not help how much of my body was exposed by the white skirt and sash, their judging eyes blamed me for every time their husbands or lovers had found warmth in another's bed. Oddly enough, even the most prudish of Mrs. Collier's friends couldn't help but ogle Thomas where he stood inconspicuously in the corner. One went so far as to tell him to serve her spirits, her eyes following the curve of his bicep when he passed her the small glass of green liqueur.

Even when their conversation turned from insipid to downright terrified, it was hard to make myself pay attention to the high whine of their feminine voices. There had been another quake, a shake so strong many felt it on the lower levels of their grand buildings. I had been oblivious to the tremors on the top floor. These women were more concerned than Jhondu's guests had been.

"Suand says it's nothing. I want to believe him, of course, but I heard there is a crack in the Sea Wall. There has never been a crack in the Wall before."

Avah was quick to wave a dismissive hand at her friend. "Veola, your husband smokes enough *ghanja* to make a pack of Wilders seem less threatening than a slave girl. His words would hardly ease my mind either." She glanced in my direction. "That being said, Xzan has seen the crack himself and he tells me they have already patched it up. It's really not so bad as the gossips are saying."

"I would rather be sent to the Wilds than have the sea sweep us away. Suand took me to the wall once. There was so much water I swear I felt as though the very air was going to drown me. They had to carry me down in a sling."

A round of tinkling laughter eased the mood and set the conversation back on a more frivolous path. I tried to imagine what it would be like, standing on a wall and seeing nothing but water stretching into the distance. I was failing. In my head, the water ended abruptly against another wall, painted to look like the sky. Now the Wilds, that I had seen. No slave lives very long without having seen the barren wasteland to the East. I let myself slip into the old memory of that day to pass the time.

I had been only six. Strange to think I still remember it so clearly.

It was shortly after the rising of the suns, Alpha already nearing its zenith while Omega still glimmered over the southern horizon. We had ridden a glass elevator all those miles towards the sky, to where a broad walkway followed the wall around the entire city. I remember my fear like the acidic aftertaste of bile in my mouth. I longed for my grandmother's comforting hand to hold. As it was, Lark was pressed bravely against the glass, his small face alight with excitement. Grey eyes turned proudly towards his father. "Look, father! Look! I see our tower!"

"Yes, Lark," Xzan had nodded absently. He was staring absently at the portable screen in his hand. Lark rolled his eyes before resuming his eager observations of the city.

When we reached the top, Xzan had had to take my hand to guide me out onto the wall. "Open your eyes, girl. I won't have you thrown from the wall, I promise."

I had opened my eyes at his command, my fear abating at the calm encouragement in my master's voice. Lark was already ahead of us. He had turned back to share his excitement with his father, but his eager face darkened at the sight of Xzan gingerly helping a slave girl from the lift. "Come on, father. I want to see the Wilds."

Together we approached the edge of the wall, my hand still firmly encased in Xzan's. Even now I'm not sure whether it was I who clung to him, or him to me. Was it because I was afraid or because Xzan didn't want me to miss the lesson he had brought me there to teach? It never occurred to me that he too might harbor some fear of the distance between us and solid ground.

At first, I had been too terrified to look over the insignificant railing holding us back from certain death. When I did, I could only admire the way the blue metallic wall stretched forever in either direction. I knew at some point it curved towards the sea to hold back its fretful waters, but what I could see of it ran straight and true. After several bated breaths, I managed to look down.

Xzan pointed to the runaway slave that had been bound to the unforgiving earth down below. I never learned if he had died there, lying against the scorched earth. Despite our distance, I could see that his skin was an angry red from the assault of the suns. There was a dark speck against his flesh. It moved, and I realized it was a single dark bird feasting on the dying flesh. I remember he had still been alive then. I was too far to see the rise and fall of his chest, or to notice if he struggled uselessly against his chains, but no distance could mute the sound of his screams. When the bird pulled a strip of flesh from his stomach, I had heard his agony float up to me; Xzan's gentle warning followed: "Those who defy their masters must pay the price in flesh."

"Look," Lark whispered. I tore my eyes away from the gruesome sight to look instead at my master's son. The boy was smiling, and his small hands twisted where he clutched the railing. "I think its going to eat his eyes next."

Surrounded again by the tittering voices of Avah's friends, I shook my head to clear the memory. My arms were covered in goosebumps. I shivered.

My eyes darted to where Thomas stood frozen in one corner. I let my eyes linger only long enough to assure myself he wasn't about to leave the room and abandon me with these women. His expression was focused on a memory of his own, lips turned down in distaste. I prayed the ladies would release me to my chambers before my own disgust began to show. Schooling my expression was getting more difficult by the moment.

Lark came in just before the ladies were getting ready to leave. He flirted with them, allowed his mother to coo and fawn over his most recent "ordeal". My legs were going numb, standing in the corner as I was, but I still felt my knees shake when his cold eyes met mine. *I think it's going to eat his eyes next.* I could never manage to look away, even if my face revealed nothing of the fear and revulsion I felt. I willed myself to lower my eyes, but my own defiance defied me. His leer was gaining venomous momentum when Thomas shifted just enough to block his view. I heard Lark's scarcely concealed growl; it was soon muffled by the rustle of robes being donned for departure. I felt even better when I watched the most forward of the women reach around to get a good grip of Thomas' ass. Her thin brows arched above her veil in what I could only assume was a show of approval. I suppressed an amused chuckle at the ball of muscle rolling around in Thomas' jaw as he clenched back angry words. When we were finally dismissed from the room, I began to fear his teeth might break from the way he ground them together.

Before I left him in the hall outside my room, I turned to offer Thomas a reassuring smile. "Don't let those old ladies get to you, Wilder. Their favours come with all sorts of perks, you know. I heard the one in red lets her pets wear her husband's clothes. They're not half as prudish as they would have others believe."

Thomas snorted, his brows drawn together in an angry scowl. "At least in the ring I knew what the masters wanted of me. Fight. Kill or be killed. Things were simpler. I was never good at the games nobility play."

I laughed, surprised by the lyrical music the sound made in my own ears. "I am not sure what nobility means where you're from, but I promise you there isn't a noble soul in the whole of Atlantis. Besides, the rules are as simple as they were before."

Thomas stepped closer, startling me with the way his hooded eyes took in the laughter on my face. "How so?"

My breath caught in my throat as I retreated a step. "Keep your head down and your mouth shut. Simple enough."

"I prefer to fight," Thomas sighed, reaching a hand up to smooth my hair off my face. It was an unnecessary gesture that set my body on fire. "I get the sense you might prefer to fight, too."

I felt trapped by his gaze, my room a safe zone just out of reach behind me. "I prefer to live," I whispered. It took every ounce of my self-control to take the final step inside. "Let me know how fighting works out for you, though," I offered with what I hoped was a playful grin to mask my fear. When the door slid shut with a soft whoosh, it took my breath right out of me. I fell back in bed, curled up on my side, and did everything I could not to dream about intense green eyes or the man they belonged to.

Chapter 12

The next two days were swept away from the mundane only in the sweet release of my Dreams. Each day I found myself longing for the chimes echoing through the apartments, alerting those who cared that it was now an acceptable time to sleep. In my Dreams – for I was sure they were more than the fantasies of normal sleep – I found myself experiencing things I could never have imagined in my desolate waking world.

The third night in my strange new Dream was just as the previous two had been. I found myself in the meadow of tall grass, surrounded by wildlife foreign even to the books I had read. Despite this, their names would appear in my mind when I needed them. It was as if I had always known their alien identities, only I had forgotten them until the moment I saw them. The billowing clouds of delicate insects were butterflies. The birds I had tried to chase were swans. I saw no other mice after the first, but I introduced myself to their robust brown cousins, with their proud fluffy tails and industrious natures, and knew them to be squirrels. The intelligent eyes watching me when I dipped my tired feet in the cool water of a pond belonged to a fox.

I collapsed on the bank laughing when I finally managed to grip the slick body of a frog I had been hunting with a good measure of delight. How such creatures came to be in *my* Dreams became a mystery I felt driven to solve. However, when I tried to explore the clearing too carefully, a song was carried to me on the wind. It would lull me into a true sleep where dreams were only dreams. If I was as free in those ordinary dreams I do not remember.

The fourth night was different for a whole other reason. The fourth night was when I discovered a way I could fly, and for the first time in my life, I knew what it felt to be free.

I was resting by the pond, idly trailing my fingers among the lily pads to lure the sleepy carp from the hidden ledges below the water. There was a rustle to my left. I pretended to ignore it, certain I would catch the dreamer whose space I was invading at last. I waited until the rustle became a splash before daring to glance up through to see who had come to join me.

The creature took my breath away.

My gaze started as it always did: from the ground. Dark, delicate hooves pranced lightly against the soft earth, pawing every so often as if to encourage me to keep looking up. I followed the slender legs to a broad chest, admiring the curving grace of its neck, until I met the liquid brown eyes oozing curiosity as they examined me in turn. I stood as slowly as I could, my eyes never leaving those of the animal. A perfect black star coiled the hair on its forehead. It was framed by tendrils of dark hairs that trailed down a long face and dipped as it nodded its head in my direction. On unsteady legs I moved forward, one hand outstretched until only the length of a spoon separated it from the velvety muzzle. The animal – the word *horse* brushed against my thoughts – was not as hesitant as I. It stepped bravely forward, nuzzling my shoulder while I inhaled the earthen perfume of its body. My hand came to rest against its neck. My skin was a dirty brown next to such a luminescent white coat. My fingers tangled themselves in the silky mane where it melted into the animal's withers, and an unspoken invitation flashed in my mind.

Before I could think too carefully about what I was doing, or how I knew how to do it, I swung my leg over the creature's back. I settled onto the curve of muscle behind its shoulders as if I had been born to sit there.

My meadow stretched out before pounding hooves as the horse took me towards a horizon too far away to see. The uncanniness of the Dream kept me glued to the animal's back, even when I dared to release my grip on the mane and throw my arms out to the side. Someone watched me, I felt it in the goosebumps rising on my skin, yet the exhilaration of wind tearing at my hair and bringing the sting of tears streaming down my cheeks made me close my eyes instead of seeking out the silent observer. Let them look at who I could be. No one could catch me now. I was flying! I was free! And if I never returned to my body again, I knew I would live out eternity in this complete happiness until my consciousness melted into the unknown.

I woke later with regretful tears soaking my pillow. I sobbed until I heard a familiar song seeping through the walls from the room next door. The rich tone of Thomas' voice was all I could make out, yet a sense of complete calm settled over me and I slept.

Thomas

Thomas felt the skin break open on his knuckles as his fifth punch crushed his opponent's jaw. The other man was done, a limp pile of muscle and rags at Thomas' feet. This would be the five-hundredth kill for Thomas. He took a haggard step back, a broken rib preventing him from fully catching his breath. The thunder of applause, the angry cries of those who had lost money on his win, were muted by the sound of his heart pounding in his ear. Despite the way his stomach recoiled inside him, Thomas forced himself to step forward again. He took the unconscious man's head in his hands and snapped his neck with one, quick twist. The audience cheered louder.

Thomas felt he had only blinked his eyes when he found himself in Alder's back room after the fight while a silent slave girl rubbed a salve that tingled against his wounds and forced his flesh to knit itself back together. His rib was bound by gauze soaked in a similar solution. Thomas took a full breath at last.

"Thank you," he murmured to the girl before she scurried away at the approach of Alder. Thomas straightened his shoulders when he saw his master was not alone.

Alder had changed in the past ten years. His skin had lightened to a soft olive complexion since he gave up searching for slaves in the Wilds. Thomas had made him too rich for such hardships. His eyes bulged from skin he had paid a surgeon to tighten each year as if his wealth might deter age itself. His robes were more colourful too, like he was trying to mimic an exotic bird, though they were nothing like ones worn by the man at his side. Thomas knew Mandar the moment he saw him. He also knew what the man wanted, what he always wanted when he came around after a fight. The sleazy lawyer had been trying to buy Thomas for years. By the look of the metal collar dangling from his sweaty hand, he had finally named a price Alder couldn't say no to.

Thomas stood so he could glare down at Mandar; he smiled when he saw the way the lawyer's jowls trembled. "You have sold me," Thomas spoke to Alder, the accusation amplified by the leftover adrenaline of the fight. "To this sack of meat."

"Is that any way to speak to your new master?" Mandar cried, his voice crackling with apprehension. Thomas' eyes silenced him. The

lawyer would learn he had not purchased a lapdog for a pet, or he would live to regret it. Thomas had teeth.

Alder chuckled. "Now, Wilder, you knew this day was coming. You've slowed down. It's almost like you don't care if you live or die in the ring anymore. You still win every fight, but you lack the passion you used to show." There was a pause in Alder's speech that drew Thomas' attention. No amount of surgeries could change a man's eyes, and in them, Thomas thought he saw the glassy beginnings of tears. Alder gave his head a shake and looked away first.

"Ten years is long enough, and the audience is bored with you," he continued as he busied himself pouring a drink from the decanter of spirits he kept to celebrate every win. The slump of his shoulders suggested this wasn't a toast to the night's win, but Thomas still couldn't shake the anger rising in his chest. "I care about you too much to cast you out into the Wilds. Better to serve out your time enjoying the luxuries of a bodyguard in a wealthy home. A fitting retirement for an undefeated champion, I think."

Thomas glared openly at both men in his presence. He wouldn't give the man who had taken him in and put him in the pit to kill or be killed the pleasure of knowing he gave a shit about going somewhere new. He'd rather die in the ring than go with the soft sack of flesh that was Mandar.

Little more was said. Mandar had a collar he intended to put on Thomas' neck, but Alder stopped him. "You won't need that," he assured the new master. To Thomas he said: "This is the best I can do for you, old friend. I won't watch your blood be spilled by the next young upstart. Enjoy your retirement."

Thomas pushed past him without acknowledging the tear that escaped the other man's eyes, or the ones burning unshed at the back of his.

An entire week was spent at his new home before Thomas set foot outside it again. He wasted time holding meditative poses meant to strengthen his core and settle his mind. He took measured breaths, balancing himself on fingers and toes for hours until his muscles were as numb as his restless emotions, yet the peace he used to find in the fighting pits eluded him. At least when he fought, when he took a rib-crunching blow or felt the little bones in his hands crack against a skull, he felt the chastising pain he deserved. The beanstalk had brought him to hell for his transgression – albeit a more glittering and ethereal hell than any priest had ever described – filled with sinful hearts blacker than his own. Now, without even his daily penance to keep his memories in check, Thomas began to dwell on the mistakes of the past and how badly he wished he could change them.

When summons came at last, Thomas resisted the urge to lunge for the freedom of the front door.

Driving through Atlantis made Thomas queasy. The hum of the car left a fuzzy feeling in his stomach; he swallowed a swirl of nausea when they turned a corner and the metal shell swayed against the momentum of its own weight and the pull of the magnets beneath it. The only thing Thomas hated more was the way the earth in this world raged against the parasitic presence of Atlantis on its back. The first time the ground had rolled beneath his feet, Thomas had spilled the contents of his stomach onto Alder's shoes. It had been so abrupt, the buildings overhead swaying like blades of grass in the wind, yet no one around him had seemed to care. They scarcely paused in their business while they waited for the ground beneath their feet to cease quivering. Alder had laughed at Thomas' unease.

Thomas pushed the memory of his first master from his mind.

The car came to a stop outside one of the tallest buildings in the city. Thomas craned his neck to look for its peak, wondering if the glittering lights overhead were stars or just the distant lights of the apartments. Broken moonlight shimmered against the metal sides and masked the subtle sway of the tower in the wind. Mandar, a sheen of sweat on his brow fit to rival the shine of the building, cleared his throat to bring Thomas' attention back to the cracked pavement beneath his feet.

The lobby of the building was as bright as the exterior was dull. Red carpets and garish blue chaises offended the senses and threatened Thomas' already weakened control of his stomach. The elevator doors were polished bronze, offering a momentary reflection of its passengers before sliding open for them. Thomas' lips quirked up at the corners when he caught sight of himself, a hairy barbarian next to Mandar huddled in the folds of his robes. The moment of humour vanished when he saw the sheer panic in those beady black eyes. In that moment, he remembered why he had been purchased in the first place and crossed heavy arms over his chest to intimidate any who might bring harm to the terrified little man in front of him.

At first, the elevator only deposited them into another foyer, different from the lobby only in its more modest display of colour. Thomas was left to wait while Mandar disappeared into the office of whoever he had come to see. He eyed the nearest chaise, wondering if the tiny woman sitting at a desk next to the office door might mind his sitting while he waited. How could he protect his master if he was left to wait outside the door? He might as well relax. The thought passed quickly, nothing more than the musing of a bored mind. Thomas jumped at the sound of the door ahead sliding into the wall.

"Go inside," the woman told him, her voice detached and her eyes never leaving the work on her desk.

Thomas obeyed, more out of curiosity than a desire to please. The door, it turned out, led down a brief hallway before a second sliding door revealed the grand office of the man they had come to see. Once upon a time, Thomas might have taken notice of the contemporary grandeur of the office, with its oversized metal desk and the barren layout of the few other pieces of furniture. Any other time he would have certainly noticed the man whose office this belonged to, if only for the austerity of his presence, but this day was different. Everything else in Thomas' world spun out of focus except for her.

She stood in a corner behind the great desk, her feet cut from the sharp edges of her pedestal, and her eyes, like pools of molten gold, challenged the presence of every man in the room. He watched her assess him, admire him even, and felt the first stirrings of his flesh at the subtle blush in her cheek when she realized he had caught her staring. He was flooded with shame when Mandar collared him before the woman's eyes and resisted the hard commands of the master when he was told to kneel.

Bolts of electricity seared the nerves in his body, casting him to the floor in convulsing agony. Even that was not enough to drive the golden-eyed woman from his thoughts. When he realized he had just been handed over to yet another master, he wanted to weep with joy. He had not been forsaken after all! This woman, this goddess of the afterlife, was as trapped as he was in the clutches of a monster. Perhaps she didn't know how her eyes begged him for freedom. He made himself a promise then: if it was the last thing he ever did, he would find it for her.

He would be her hero.
She would be his redemption.

Chapter 13

"I hate wearing the same thing again and again," Thomas grumbled while watching me fuss with my makeup applicator from the doorway. He picked at an invisible thread on his kilt with distaste. "Where I come from, there are colours and pageantry and celebrations of identity. You can tell the make of a man simply by the colours he wears."

"Then how is it that you managed to lose yourself in the Wilds? If home was such a fabulous place to be, why wander off at all?" There was a little snap in my voice, vestigial bitterness from losing the dream I had been enjoying so much the night before.

Thomas crossed his arms and leaned against the doorframe. "Foolishness. I thought I had something to prove. Turns out there's something to be said for being content with what you have."

I nodded, absently adjusting my skirt so the seams lined up with the outside of my thighs. I felt a strange ache in my muscles from riding, another side-effect from the experiences one could have in the Dream.

I could still feel Thomas watching me. "Are you content, Bella?"

When I turned to look at him, my eyes were suitably widened to feign offence at such a question. Not to mention the use of the nickname he had given me where he could be overheard. I no longer needed the continual gestures to remind him of the cameras in every room; it turned out he just didn't care who heard him. *Am I content?* There was no way for me to mouth the answer Xzan would expect of a loyal slave. I couldn't bring myself to even try. I *had* been content once. At least, I thought I had.

Now the idea of freedom was seeping into my mind like sewage from a backed-up pipe. It polluted everything I thought I knew or felt; Xzan's small kindnesses over the years now dug into my skin, barbs of falsehoods I couldn't shed no matter how I might want to. I realized I had thought Xzan might care for me, like a precious artifact worth protecting. The idea I was no more than a tool, though valuable, discoloured any fond memories I had held on to through the years.

This life was not enough. This life was a fallacy I could tolerate no more.

For several minutes, I wallowed in self-pity and imagined riding that strange horse into the Wilds until I fell off the end of the earth. That is, until Thomas cleared his throat.

"What are you doing here, anyway?" I snapped, my cheeks burning at the idea the strange man might have read my mind.

A dark look passed over Thomas' eyes, a shadow of anger soon replaced by cool indifference. "Just looking out for you. I've been told I'm in charge of your safety every day, all day. They don't even close my door at night. That Collier brat must be a real piece of work."

My breath caught in my throat, stopped by all the things I should have said to defend my master's family. Instead, I only nodded. The exhaustive nature of my unease was expelled by a heavy sigh. "Perhaps you can keep watch from *outside* my door. I would like to be alone for a little while."

Thomas hesitated, his brows coming together over the bridge of his nose in an expression I had already determined was his version of thoughtful. In the end, he only bowed his head, an honourable gesture I would never have imagined offered to me, and managed a soft, "As you wish, my lady," before the door slid closed.

In that moment, if my head wasn't already a mess of contradicting thoughts, I might have noticed the subtle flutter of my heart when I imagined Thomas on the other side of the door watching over me. I might have indulged the fantasy of his lips uttering my name in a whisper meant to soothe my very soul. Instead, I lay back in my bed, hugging my pillow to my chest while I tried to clear my mind of rebellious thoughts. I closed my eyes and hummed the tune of the breeze in my dreams.

I had almost achieved some sense of peace when the room began to shake.

It started slowly at first, a slight shiver, a soft rumble. I sat up, my eyes traveling to the quivering water in the toilet bowl. Then the earth shook in earnest. I was pitched from the bed, bruising my knees on the hard metal of the floor before I could right myself enough to clutch the side of my bed. The door slid open – it was designed to open during a quake, but no quake had ever been strong enough to make it happen – and I crawled clumsily towards the opening. Thomas was there to meet me, his face a startling shade of green and his stance even more unsteady than mine. I touched his arm, meaning to tell him not to worry, when the mirror on my wall crashed to the floor and shattered. I let out a startled cry and pulled my body into a tight little ball in the shelter of the doorway.

A heavy body wrapped itself around me, pulling me into the warmth of something more stable than the floor beneath me. I melted into it, trying to hum my little tune until the thundering of the earth's tantrum abated.

When everything stilled once more, I remained frozen. Fear of the aftershocks seemed to have paralyzed me.

Thomas was the first to speak, his voice shaking with the effort it took to hide the lingering queasiness in his stomach. "Are you alright?"

I pulled back my head to look towards him. His body was curled around mine, strong arms braced against the floor on either side of me. One hand had come down on a shard of the mirror and was bleeding. He didn't seem to notice. "I think so, but you're bleeding," my voice faltered when those piercing green eyes did not so much as glance at the crimson puddle his hand was creating.

"That was a big one," his voice still shook despite his attempt at a light-hearted tone. His shaggy hair curled from the moisture on his brow and teased the skin of my forehead.

"Yeah," I agreed. "I've never felt it so strongly up here before. The buildings were designed to absorb the motion." I shivered.

When Thomas stood, I felt the rush of fresh air, free of his masculine scent, like a slap to the face. He offered me his good hand to help me stand. "If there is one thing that's true in both my world and yours, it's that Nature can be an ornery bitch when she's upset with you."

"Who is Nature?" I asked, puzzled by the term I had never heard used in such a context. Nature was the inclinations of a man or a woman, the aspects of their souls to which I shaped their Dreams.

"She's not really a 'who'," Thomas tried to explain. "Nature is the earth: the animals and the trees and the weather. Those types of things."

"But you called it a 'she'," I pushed.

"Aye. The earth gives us life like a woman gives life to her children, so we call Nature a 'she'."

I remembered the desolation of the Wilds, the desert that stretched out as far as the eye could see. In my mind, I conjured up my little dream-meadow: the clouds of butterflies, the clever fox, the cool water of the pond and all its mysteries. "We don't have Nature here," I concluded. I saw agreement in Thomas' pinched expression. "Perhaps we have already killed her."

"I have to agree," Thomas said. A shadow passed over his face. "I've seen many men die, I've been responsible for most of those deaths, and there are some who fight death even after their heart has stopped pumping their lifeblood into the ground. They thrash and twist until you're sure they have been possessed by some terrible spirit. It seems to me Nature means to tear you all down with her before she gives in to her own end."

We stood in silence, so close our bodies might touch if we took a large enough breath. We were leagues apart in our somber thoughts. It wasn't until I noticed the congealed blood on my floor that I remembered Thomas' hand. I took it in mine, opening the palm to get a better look. It wasn't as bad as I thought. A small shard of glass was protruding from a cut no wider than his thumb. Gingerly stepping around the debris on my floor, I took him into my room to clean the wound at my sink.

As I worked, I felt his breath against my neck. The heat of it set my skin on fire and made it hard to concentrate on the task. "Belladonna," he whispered. A strange sensation that had been building in my stomach travelled to lower regions. My fingers spasmed where they wiped blood from his palm. If I kissed him there, would it be so wrong?

But this wasn't the Dream.

The sounds of someone approaching down the hall drove us apart in the space of a breath. Still, when I closed my eyes, I imagined what such pleasures would feel like in the flesh.   With his breath still tingling against the back of my neck, Thomas resumed his place outside my door, and I was left alone with the eyes of my shattered reflection staring up at me from the floor.

Chapter 14

If Lark attempted to access my room after the quake, I never heard any commotion to prove it. In fact, the only distraction I had the whole day was Red appearing briefly with a change of clothes and instructions to leave my hair loose. She swept up the mess of my mirror and supervised the hanging of a new one before I was alone again. The skirt she left was fashioned more like a wrapped kilt, held in place by a fine satin sash. The top made me curl my lip in distaste. Long sleeves, decorated in small white beads hugged my arms right up over my shoulders, where they met a tight band of fabric I could only describe as a collar.

That was it.

Not a stitch of clothing had been left for me save the sandals on my feet. My breasts, still high and firm in testimony to my youth, were heavy enough to feel uncomfortable without the support offered by my usual sash. It was hard not to immediately cover myself when the door to my room slid open again. As it turned out, seeing Thomas made the instinct stronger. I found myself desperate to put more clothes on. The fact he had the decency to blush and look away went a long way to return a modicum of modesty to the situation.

"I guess we're a matching set tonight," he observed, adjusting the sash of his own kilt. The partial shirt he wore matched my own, though I doubted the fabric of mine protested the way his did; his muscles seemed too big for the slim sleeves. I thought about the way he had wrapped his body around me earlier and knew the fabric would tear should he do it now.

"As long as I only wear one collar," I replied, cringing when I watched his fingers brush against where cold metal was hidden by the collar of his "shirt". It was easy to forget the ex-fighter wore such a thing. Very few slaves ever had before.

I felt a blush rise to my own cheeks when I realized my eyes had begun to travel freely over Thomas' body. It was a beautiful thing to behold, wild and untamed as it was. There was a small kernel of envy blossoming inside when I acknowledged the strength such a body must possess. *At least my breasts are nicer,* I thought to myself with a smile. I had a sudden urge to feel the hair on his chest, to press my face against it to see if it was as soft as it looked.

Thomas' mouth did that odd twitch I thought might be the precursor to a grin, yet he held it in check. "If you ask me, you are the more dangerous of the two of us."

"And what could possibly make you decide that?" I challenged, stepping out into the hall.

"I'm good at reading people."

I looked up at him. I am tall for a woman, at least as tall as Xzan, so I reached Thomas' shoulders. Still, it felt as though I had to strain my neck to meet his eyes. "So am I. In fact, give me half a chance and I could tell you every dream you've ever had."

The sorrow, always churning just below the surface, flooded his eyes until he looked away. "That would be too easy."

"Why?"

When he met my eyes again, I thought there was the shine of tears in his eyes. "Because I've only ever had one."

I cocked my head to one side. "What dream is that?"

Another twitchy smile. "To go home."

I hardly had time to process Thomas' words before we were summoned to the sitting room where the family had gathered. I tucked them away in the back of my mind to consider later.

When we entered the sitting room, Mrs. Collier was the first to draw my eye. She was a walking coat rack, all but her eyes completely covered by red and purple silk. Ropes of silver were draped here and there to give her the illusion of a figure. The men were less 'conservative' by Atlantian standards, settling instead on loose shirts and fitted leggings in black. Xzan brightened his ensemble with a shimmering lavender robe and matching boots. Lark's outfit stayed suitably somber to match his mood. Before he noticed our arrival, he was glaring sullenly at the floor with a glass of liquor brought partway to his lips. Whatever thoughts he harboured behind the distant stare, I could sense a tension more tangible than the air before a storm.

When Thomas followed me into the room there was a muffled cry from somewhere inside Mrs. Collier's outfit; Lark struggled to cover the fact he had almost choked on his drink. Lark was a hair taller than his father, but it counted for little next to Thomas. I realized our outfits, designed as they were, served to enhance the formidable appearance of my guard. While I had wasted time on admiration, a touch of fear seemed to trickle forth from the careful control the Collier family held over their emotions.

"It is appropriate to have a guard at such an event," Xzan informed the family in response to an unasked inquiry. Still, his eyes took us in with sincere disapproval. Xzan tried to deflect the anxiety building in the room with an angry query of his own. "Why are they dressed like this?"

"If they are coming then they should be dressed appropriately for the occasion. I had no idea you were bringing the *savage* with us when I asked for the clothing to be made," Mrs. Collier informed her husband after clearing her throat. Speaking seemed to jolt her back into awareness; she made a sweeping escape towards the door. "I should think you would like your pet covered in such finery. I suppose it is much more appropriate if the pair of them at least match."

Xzan either agreed with his wife or made the strategic decision not to argue. With matters of society, Avah was the one in charge; Xzan was wise to make no further comment. He let his wife and son lead the way from the room before sweeping out ahead of Thomas and myself. I held my head held as proudly as I could manage with my eyes downcast as I followed obediently behind them.

The ride across town was silent. When he thought his father wasn't looking, Lark shuffled closer to me so he could stare openly. His hand came up once to brush an imaginary strand of hair away from my neck. When he caught Thomas watching his fingers hovering over my exposed flesh, he altered his intentions. Unfortunately, my body's response did more to encourage the game of cat and mouse being played between the two men. While Lark had to wait for his father to look elsewhere, there was nothing Thomas could do when Lark managed an accidental fondling while leaning across me for a better window view. I let my mind carry me away from the stifling tension of the vehicle; it was the only defense I had. At long last we pulled up to another high rise.

The family got out first to the bright flash of camera lights. I climbed out in their shadow, staying out of sight as much as I could. A collectively indrawn breath told me Thomas had joined us. While the media were trained to ignore the presence of the help, such as we were, Thomas made an imposing sight as he eyed each of them as though they were potential threats. The lights were followed by questions shouted from every direction.

"Mr. Collier, is it true new witnesses have come forward in the Banderos Massacre?"

"Is it true you bribed the judge during the original trial?"

"Mr. Lark, is it true you were assaulted by an opposing gang while in Dungeon?"

For the most part, the family proceeded indoors without so much as nodding in a reporter's direction. The closer we got to the doors, the more serious the media members became.

"Mr. Collier, how has your son's criminal trial affected your relationship with the Mayor?"

Xzan laughed. "Well, I'm at his party, aren't I? I should think the Mayor believed, as I did, in the due diligence of our justice system. My son was innocent. We are just like everyone else in this city: guilty until proven otherwise. We are just glad justice was served and our son is home again. Excuse us, please."

Once inside, the facade was dropped. The excess outer garments were taken from Mrs. Collier until she wore only a simple gown and turban. From the lobby, we were led into a large conference room filled with people. It was dimly lit by small globes of light hanging from the high ceiling. Slaves and paid servants alike danced here and there with trays of drinks or food for all the guests in attendance. Real food, even. Small cakes and strange little fish dipped in a white sauce. Though none would ever pass my lips, I stared at it all in wonder. The food cubes people ate most of the time met our nutritional needs, made to fill our stomachs and satisfy our tastes without the time needed to prepare and consume a meal, or the scarce natural resources required, but real food was something else entirely. The very idea of it was a rare treat afforded only to the wealthiest members of society.

I felt better about my appearance when I saw other slaves accompanying their masters. They were all in various forms of costumed dress, though even those permitted to hide their face wore little more than a square of fabric to hide their most secret parts. Next to some I felt positively overdressed. I decided the best thing I could do was stay close to Xzan while he made his introductory rounds. Not only would it put a safe distance between Lark and my breasts, it seemed a practical way to spend the evening. He was my master. I was his shadow. It was the purpose I served, available to use my gift whenever necessary.

For some reason, this was more difficult than usual.

From the conversations I overheard, I knew this was a celebration of sorts. The mayor had been sworn in for a second term, running unopposed as was often the case when one was nominated by Xzan Collier himself. Overhearing conversations was only so helpful in a room as noisy as the one we found ourselves in. Where I gleaned the most information was typically in my ability to watch people. Slaves weren't supposed to let their eyes travel much higher than a master's waist, but I had a reputation that afforded me somewhat more freedom. I could dare to look higher. Most of the time, no one even noticed me staring – I could note the smile that lacked sincerity, the grimace that hid in the corners of the eyes, or the hand that reached up to tug softly at a collar as easily as I could find the door to people's dreams – but when they did I could feign embarrassment through fluttering lashes and almost, but not quite, lowered eyes. For most that was enough, a little flirting and all was forgiven. For others, what could they really do about it anyway? I was the property of the Colliers and there was nothing they could do about the insult.

Since it turned out there was very little to learn from those we met as Xzan made his way through the room, he eventually grabbed a servant by the arm and told him to take me and Thomas somewhere until we were called for. I was grateful to leave the noise behind.

We were not alone in the room we were led to. Other slaves had been left to wait for the whims of their masters in a lounge off the main room. Couches had been arranged for them to sit on, and trays of little coloured cubes were set out on low tables with decanters of sweetened water. Some of the others in the room were indulging in the illusion of freedom, laughing quietly together in small, huddled groups, or scattering themselves throughout the room. Regardless of who they spoke to or where they sat, there was no illusion as to which families were allied to others. Not a word of truth was spoken from a single mouth, I was sure, for each and every one of the men and women before us was a spy for their master. There was no other reason for them to be there. Thomas and I stayed close to each other, finding a quiet corner where we could watch the room, including the entrance, but have enough privacy to talk if we chose.

For a while we didn't speak at all. It was too much of a relief to be away from the overwhelming din of the larger celebration. After a while, I began to fidget in my seat, anxious to be done with whatever my task would be that night. I turned to Thomas, raising my voice only enough for it to reach his ears.

"Where is home?"

Thomas didn't answer at first, making me think he hadn't heard me. "Camelot," he said at last.

"Is that in the Wilds?"

Thomas shook his head. "No. I think Camelot might not be part of this world at all."

I raised an eyebrow. "What do you mean?"

His green eyes were closer to amber in the dim light. "I'm not sure I can explain it. I'm no longer sure I even believe my own story anymore."

"Try me," I dared, anxious to pass the time with something more interesting than the gossip I could hear from the other groups. Besides, the lilting accent in his voice was a song I could listen to all night.

Thomas took a deep breath. "When I was younger, almost fifteen years ago now, I took something from a defeated enemy. I wanted to find a place where I could be the hero, where people would know my name and sing stories about the great deeds I could accomplish." He paused to shake his head. "Odd to think I ended up in a place where I am not even permitted to have a name."

"You gave me one," I pointed out, refusing to look away when his eyes searched mine for the sincerity of my gratitude.

"I just reminded you that you had one," his smile parted his lips.

Before I could dwell too long on the soft pout of his lower lip, I urged him to go on with his story.

"The objects I took created some kind of opening from my world to yours. When I reached this side, I hardly had time to get my feet under me before the slavers caught me in my sleep. The two suns, the broken moon...I thought I had died and been left to wander purgatory for my sins. When the slavers got me, I knew I must be in some sort of hell. Where I come from, men fight to gain status or to defend the weak. Here, I had to fight to survive because they only fed me when I won. I knew I was being punished for what I had done back home, and I began to welcome the pain I experienced in the pits every day."

I swallowed a lump in my throat. "What did you do? I mean, what did you do back in your world to deserve such punishment?"

"Murder."

He fell silent and I let his words sink in. I had blood on my hands too, and likely for less cause than the tormented man next to me. What punishment did I deserve? Did it matter that I had killed on the command of another? *Except for Hal,* I reminded myself. No, I refused to think of it that way. I couldn't. Instead, I turned my focus back to the more fantastic element of his story.

He came from another world. Was it possible? It had to be. What was the Dream if not another world? The more I thought about it, the more excited I became. My heart raced in my chest while a thousand possibilities raced through my mind. "Are there slaves in your world?"

Thomas stared at me openly until I returned his gaze. "You believe me?"

I wondered if at that moment I looked as vulnerable as he did. "I have secrets that are equally unbelievable but no less true."

"And what about my crimes?" his voice deepened with the echoes of his regret.

I tried to laugh away the seriousness of his confessions. "Have you forgotten how you got this job?"

Thomas waited the space of a breath, his lips twitching at the corners. "No," he replied at last. "There are no slaves. Not like this. Even the lowliest serf has the protection of his lord or king. It is not a perfect system, but it is better than this. There was some abuse of power – such abuses seem to be part of all humanity – but the knights are sworn to uphold the king's law and bring such wrongdoers to justice."

"Are knights like the authorities here?"

"Yes, I should think so," Thomas laughed dryly. "Equally as corrupt, too. The knights were meant to represent the ideal protector of the innocent, except after a while anyone with the money to buy a horse could buy a place at the round table."

His bitterness shocked me. It oozed off his tongue with enough acid to distract me from the fact I had only recently discovered what a horse was and where I discovered such information. "Did you want to be a knight?"

"Yes."

"Then why didn't you stay and become one? Perhaps you could have changed things for the better."

"I tried," Thomas confessed. "I thought I was doing just that. I was told of a lady, held captive by a hideous beast. I went to save her. As it turned out, by saving her I handed her over to someone even worse."

"Who?"

"My brother, Jack."

We lapsed into silence again. There was a table in front of us with ENSA cubes and a decanter of liqueur. I poured us each a cup, draining my own before Thomas could finish his. "You saved her from one monster and gave her to another."

Thomas stared sadly into his glass. "Yes."

I poured myself another draught. Disappointment had settled heavily on my chest. "Perhaps our worlds are not so different."

If Thomas intended to reply to my observation, he was not given the chance. Lark had appeared at the entrance, giving orders to the first servant who bobbed at attention. The young man ended up scurrying over to where we sat.

"Your master requires your presence," he spoke only to me. When Thomas moved to stand with me, the other man held up a hand. "Your master said he would send for you separately."

I looked back to where Lark waited. He was twirling something casually in his hand; it was the control to Thomas' collar. Lark raised his eyebrows as if to ask: *got the picture? Disobey now and the Wilder will get it.* I turned to Thomas, daring to put a reassuring hand on his arm. "I'll be fine," I told him before rising to walk away with a confidence I wasn't feeling.

Lark's smile slid into a slimy grin when he saw I had left my protection behind. "My father wants his sweet little prize."

I walked ahead of Lark as if I knew exactly where I was going. Head up, eyes down, haughty in the face of Lark's contempt but not truly doing anything wrong. He was content to follow for a while, whether for the view or for the amusing prospect of me getting lost I could only guess. It didn't take long for him to take control. His hand gripped my arm hard enough to bruise, hurrying me along the outside of the main party room until we were in an abandoned hallway with several doors leading off into private dining rooms. We were headed for one near the end of the hall. Before he could press the sensor to announce our arrival, Lark suddenly grabbed me by the throat and pinned me against the wall. The wind was knocked out of me by the force of his surprise attack. His hand around my throat squeezed just hard enough to make regaining oxygen almost impossible. Almost. He knew exactly what he was doing.

"Do you see now?" he asked, his hot breath burning my face. "Without my father around you are no different than any other slave." His free hand thrust itself up my skirt, fingers finding the right hold to pull me against him.

"Let go of me and I can show you just how different I am," I croaked, my hands gripping his wrist though not fighting him.

Lark hesitated, curiosity doing battle with his resentment. He took his hand from my skirt and loosened his grip on my throat enough to let fresh air trickle in. "You'd like that, wouldn't you?" he smiled triumphantly. He brought his face close enough for me to feel his cheek against mine. His breath filled my ear. "I promise it won't be long. Father dearest won't be around forever. All men die someday. Some men die sooner than others."

When he stepped back, I tried not to give him the satisfaction of gulping at air now so easy to inhale. The first few breaths burned my throat. I wondered if there would be bruises on my neck, dark purple marks to tell the story of Lark's abuse. Then I wondered if Xzan, for all his special treatment, would even care. While I caught my breath, Lark swiped a hand through his short hair and straightened out his clothes. When we were both presentable again, Lark buzzed the door and ushered me in.

I could tell by the way Xzan watched the door expectantly he had not intended for Thomas to be left behind. I recognized the man he was talking to immediately and knew why I was called.

"You may leave now, Lark," Xzan told his son firmly. "Your mother was looking for you."

Lark glared at his father with more hatred than I had ever seen from him before. Had I the time then I might have pondered this, but as it was Xzan flicked a switch to dim the lights and I knew it was time to work. From hidden speakers around the room, slow, hypnotic music began to fill the air. I had a job to do. The mayor trembled with anticipation. He had a round face, though not necessarily plump, and his eyes glittered with too much drink while he watched me sashay towards him. Xzan watched me as well. His face was filled with a mix of admiration, pride, and more than a little desire. He had never touched me, not once in the way men seemed to want to touch their slaves when in a locked room, but the desire was there; it was carefully repressed behind his mask of control. I tried to remember the last time he had been a part of my work and couldn't. This thought distracted me for a reason I couldn't name.

"Congratulations, Mr. Mayor," I purred, leaning over to rest my hands on his thighs. His eyes were lingering a few inches lower than my face, so I pressed my advantages by continuing to sway with the music. "I hope you're enjoying yourself, Mr. Mayor. I would very much like to help you enjoy yourself." While I spoke, I climbed into his lap, straddling him on the couch. I used one hand to fan the flames of desire beneath his robe while the other traced the contours of his face. At last, his eyes locked with mine, the pupils dilating while his eyelids drooped lower and lower. When he was there, in that state of partial awareness, I whispered in his ear. "Where do you want me?"

The mayor had a vivid imagination, I had to give him that.

We were both naked, swimming around each other in a seemingly endless body of water lit from below by an invisible light source. The mayor himself had shed excess fat for the lean muscles of youth; it must be how he remembered himself from younger days. The water was just warm enough to be both refreshing and comfortable, and for a while I reveled in the weightlessness of swimming. The mayor laughed, floating beside me and taking pleasure in my playfulness. His whimsy was infecting me, taking away my control of the Dream. I splashed water at him before diving under to get away. In his Dream, we didn't need to come up for air. He caught me and held me suspended beneath the surface, exploring my body with hands that were surprisingly gentle. I decided to enjoy it for a while, pressing myself against him when his arousal became persistent enough to be of use. I wrapped my legs around him, letting the rhythm of the water do the work. Just as we were both approaching climax, a disembodied voice filled the Dream.

What's taking so long?

It was Xzan, whispering in the ear of my physical self. The mayor continued his climb towards release, unaware of another presence intruding on my mind. I had to regain my control, pulling back from my own pleasure enough to harness the Dream. When I knew the mayor's mind was in my grasp, I began to whisper Xzan's instructions aloud, weaving them into the dreamer's subconscious until he would have no choice but to heed them when waking.

"You will shut down the Public Trade Act. The sale of slaves in the private sector ensures the safety of all citizens by maintaining the proper channels of power."

While I gave my instructions, who to give tax breaks to, who to fire and who to hire, I thought about the Public Trade Act. It stood to reason a publicly run slave trade could balloon out of control, leading to more slaves instead of fewer. It would also make the astute businessman, one who owned most of the auction houses in town, feel a tighter pinch in his wallet. The balance of power gave me pause. More slaves reduced prices which would reduce profit. More slaves reduced power. That was a new concept to consider. If we outnumbered the masters, what power would they truly ever have? The Dream began to shiver, altering reality under the strain of my distraction. Creating a copy of myself for the mayor to keep playing with, I pulled myself away until I sat heavily in my own body.

"You seemed to be enjoying yourself," Xzan remarked when I stood from the sleeping mayor. I kept my head down, hoping the dim lighting hid the blush in my cheeks. Xzan grabbed me roughly, pulling me against him and raising my chin to look at him. I was paralyzed by fear when I saw the dull burn of jealousy in his eyes. "Do you always enjoy it so much?"

"No, I," I gasped. "It's not real when I'm in the Dream."

"It is as real as *you* want it to be," Xzan growled, shoving me back from him towards the door. "We're going. Now!"

I hardly dared to breathe until we were back in the car heading home. Thomas eyed me uncertainly, but I was making a conscious effort not to look anywhere but the floor. His hand was next to me on the seat, his little finger creeping over mine to offer comfort. I did not pull away, glad for at least that much.

Xzan marched into the building without even a glance back, leaving his wife and son to catch up to him. Lark was thoroughly amused by the whole thing. "The old man is finally getting jealous," he remarked casually, falling back to walk next to me. "About time he admitted to having a hard on for his little plaything."

Mrs. Collier stopped just outside the door and spun on her son. Or so I thought. Angry words came out in furious sputters until the full force of them landed with her palm across my cheek.

"You are a filthy creature!" she spat. "Stay away from my son or I will see you sold at the next auction." An empty threat, of course, but it seemed to mollify her. She turned and marched after her husband, leaving Lark to chase after her with words of apology.

If it wasn't for Thomas ushering me forward, I may have stood on the street lost in the shock of the evening until the next sunrise. We were alone in the lobby, the family having already boarded an elevator upstairs. One of the building staff motioned us over to a service elevator, programming our stop before stepping off to make sure we got where we were supposed to go. Once we were alone, listening to the whiz of each floor pass us by, Thomas took my hand properly, giving it a good squeeze when a tear managed to find its way down my reddened cheek. He stood silently while more tears fell, none quite giving way to sobs, only releasing my hand once the elevator slowed so I might have a chance to wipe the streaks from my face. I could see by my reflection in the metallic doors that I was more collected than I felt.

The elevator let off in the slave quarters where Red and a half dozen other men and women lived when not serving the masters. They eyed our presence with suspicion. We were like them but not them. I had never considered the way I had been set apart from them before. Red, perhaps still remembering the child I had been, smiled at me when we passed. The others showed only a mixture of distrust and disgust. I had no peers. I was alone and now even the safety of the master's preference was no longer a comfort. I wasn't even aware we had made it to my room until the whir of the door sliding open caught my attention.

"Good night," I muttered in Thomas' general direction, preparing to leave him standing in the hallway. His hand reached to clasp mine, pulling me back towards him. Before I could open my mouth to protest his lips came down on mine. I didn't resist, not even for a second. The vehemence of the initial kiss melted into something softer; I gave in to it completely. I never realized how much I had wanted him to kiss me until I was losing myself to the sensations blossoming in my gut. The scratch of his short beard against my face, and the smell of sweat and masculinity wafting off his body, made everything I had ever experienced in the

Dream no more than a distant fantasy. This was real and I didn't want it to end.

When he pulled away, we were both panting slightly. "You are it," he whispered against my hair, pulling me into the shelter of his arms. My head fit in the curve where his shoulder met his chest as if it were meant to rest there forever. "You're the reason I'm here. I wanted to prove myself, to right the wrongs of my past, and I was delivered here to you."

"I don't really know what you mean," I mumbled against his chest. His hair *was* soft against my cheek; his heart thumped as quickly as my own.

His arms squeezed tighter. "I'm going to get you away from here."

I pulled back, alarm discolouring the brief moment of contentment I had felt. "There *is* nowhere else. Runaway slaves are beaten and humiliated. Runaway slaves who steal? They are the ones decorating the city walls for the beasts of the Wilds to feast upon."

Thomas cupped my face in his hands. "You are not a possession I can steal. You are a woman, as free as you choose to be. I am asking you to come with me."

I lost myself in the tempest of his eyes, counting the flecks of gold to stop myself from seeing the sincerity of his promise. "I don't know how. Even now they watch us." My eyes darted to the cameras overhead.

Thomas ignored the hint. "I will get us away from here if you ask, but I will do nothing until you ask it of me. If you never wish to leave this place, at least remember this: I will protect you from these monsters any way that I can."

He stepped away from me then. I realized we had been on the threshold of my room the entire time. Once he was clear of the door, it slid shut. Even with him out of sight, his serious face filled my vision, engulfing me in something I had never felt before. Hope blossomed in my heart. Images of something better than this dull, metallic life infiltrated my dreams. Suddenly, I wanted to escape. I never wanted to see the four walls of my room ever again.

That night I dreamed of an open field under a warm sun. This time when I felt eyes watching me, I turned to see Thomas waiting for me, calling my name.

Chapter 15

I was left alone for days. At least, it felt like days. The monotonous hours of my life were interrupted only by ENSA cubes appearing on a tray a couple of times a day, the need to use the toilet, or the need to sleep. I heard Thomas coming and going several times. I began to realize the full reality of my new Dreams. I also began to crave them. I was using my gift while I slept without fully understanding how I did it, or why my Dream behaved so differently than the Dreams of others. One difference was that though Thomas really was there too, it seemed he had been pulled into my Dream instead of me entering his. Another difference was my lack of control. I thought perhaps I didn't truly want to be in charge. I enjoyed the reflection of Thomas' world too much to interfere with my own tainted thoughts.

In our Dream, Thomas told me about the goings-on of the house. Xzan was going to all the mayor's public events, keeping an eye on how well his puppet was performing. He was not the most powerful man in the city because he left things up to chance. I soon tired of hearing about it at all; I was already familiar with the practices of my master. In the Dream, I was more anxious to discover what freedom would mean if I ever dared to take Thomas' offer.

In the Dream, Thomas began to show me more of his world. We wandered thick forests, walking barefoot on soft carpets of moss. We tracked the musky scent of a fearsome creature he called a boar, while goofy hounds gamboled around us with their raucous cries of excitement. By far my favourite game to play was when Thomas tried to explain what a particular creature was while I tried to create it from the images in my head. With Thomas' influence, I soon found myself surrounded by every manner of animal or bird, an eagle on my shoulder and a lion at my feet. He was careful to explain the dangers of such beasts in real life, but in my Dreams they bowed to my will as I had always bowed to the will of my master. I respected the power I had over them.

We played our game, we carried on our conversations, but never did Thomas ask of me what I would have gladly given. He was clothed in a loose tunic of coarse wool and fitted leather leggings. From a description he gave me, I found myself wearing a simple gown of a similar rough fabric. It was modest and hid my figure well. Despite being fully clothed in the Dream, I had never wanted Thomas more. I think he wanted it, too, judging by the way I caught his eyes watching me in our moments of silence. When the temptation to act on our desires grew strong, I reminded myself that this wasn't real. We were in the Dream. What I wanted with Thomas needed to be real, for both of us. Otherwise, what seemed to be growing between us would be no different than any other Dreamer I had been with.

Finally, on what I estimated as the fourth day, someone came. It was not the someone I was hoping for.

I woke in the morning from a private dream, one I blushed to imagine sharing with Thomas, to the sound of the neighbouring door opening and closing. I assumed Thomas would be gone most of the day, accompanying Xzan on a trip to City Hall or some other political endeavor. Breakfast appeared. Although the ENSA cubes transformed into the creamy sweetness of milk and honey on my tongue, I chewed with annoyed impatience instead of savouring the flavour. After arranging myself as if I had been summoned already, I paced. Four steps could take me from one side of the room to the other in the longest section. Back and forth, trying desperately to quell the anxious energy building up inside of me. I jumped at the sound of my door opening behind me. When I turned, I felt the blood drain out of my face.

Lark stood there, his shirt unbuttoned down the front, his feet bare where they appeared from the bottom of his leggings. There was a new light in his eyes, warming them the way Xzan's could be warmed when he looked at me; only, it wasn't fondness lighting the fire.

"Not the favourite anymore, are you?"

I didn't answer; I was too frightened to even remember to lower my eyes. If Lark noticed he didn't care. Instead, he took a step into my room. I tried to back-up, but I hit my heel against the far wall after the first step. I stood up straighter to hide the quiver in my knees.

"I want you to come with me. Now."

He turned to leave, pausing only to make sure I followed. I didn't know what to do. To openly disobey him would result in punishment even if Xzan might privately agree with my rebellion. Xzan wouldn't want me alone with Lark. I knew it and so did the man in front of me now. He also knew his father was away for the day and there was no one around to stop him from flogging me right where I stood if I stayed where I was. I followed. Lark smiled and kept moving, so sure of my obedience he didn't even glance over his shoulder to make sure I was still there. I felt sick. Sick with fear and absolute loathing.

We ended up in his private sitting room. It felt crowded with a long curving sofa taking up almost two walls, and a well-stocked bar against a third. There were no windows in this room. I felt my chest tighten with each breath. After locking the door, Lark all but shoved me into the center of the room where a small rectangular stage had been set up. It was covered in plush cushions. I eyed the platform but did not step up onto it. Lark did not press me to try. Instead, he took it upon himself to make us drinks. I couldn't see exactly which bottle filled our glasses with clear liquid, but when he passed it to me, the smell made my breath catch in my throat.

"Drink."

A command not a request. This was *his* game, *his* rules. The residual anger, always buried somewhere inside of me, rose to the challenge. I swallowed the contents of the glass before my tongue could feel the burn of it, blinking to control the tears welling up in response. Lark's smile broadened when he took a single sip of his own.

"You promised me something," he remarked casually, backing up until he could sit comfortably on his sofa. He watched me over the rim of his glass. "You said if I got you alone, I could see just how *special* you are."

I swallowed the lump forming in my throat. "It doesn't work that way."

Lark raised a dark eyebrow. "No?" He revealed a control screen in the armrest of his seat. A few punched icons later and music began to float in the air around us. It was not what I was used to, but the steady beats of a drum served as a primal rhythm for my body to follow. I kept still, my eyes never leaving his. With a sigh, Lark shook his head, punching more buttons on his control panel.

"I really didn't want to have to reveal my hand so early, but," he watched my face when a transparent screen appeared between us. It was the video feed from outside my room. I couldn't stop my hands from clenching into fists when I saw the footage play on a loop before me.

"What is it you are trying to say?" I couldn't quite keep the anger from my voice. If anything, it amused Lark further.

"If you think my father will be upset if I fuck you right here on the floor," he sneered. "What do you think he will do when he sees you wrapped around that savage? No need to think about it, because I'm going to tell you." He paused for dramatic effect, sipping at his drink until I wanted to scream. "He will hang your lover from the city walls. He will make you watch while beasts eat his flesh. And, when death finally grants the savage mercy, my father will be happy to let me have you for myself. Believe me, slave girl, I will not tolerate insolence the way my father has."

I took several calming breaths, schooling my face into careful indifference while tears threatened to spill down my cheeks. *Not in front of this man,* I commanded myself. The truth was that five days earlier I would have called Lark's bluff. Xzan would never lower himself to such petty revenge. Thomas and I would be flogged, sure, separated, certainly, but both of us had too much value to waste on beasts of any kind. However, the jealousy I had seen after the mayor's party floated with terrifying clarity in my mind's eye.

There were no options now.

I was trapped.

I could give myself to the monster before me and show him every pleasure I had ever found in a man's mind, but my heart told me this would not be the end. He would still hold the video looping in front of us, still dangle it in front of me anytime I thought to say no in the future. *He is a threat as long as he lives,* I decided. I allowed my hips to sway in time to the drums.

"That's better." Lark vanished the video feed so he could see me properly.

I let my hair down, teasing it with my hands until it fell in suggestive waves around my body. My eyes never left his, not once, even as he raked his gaze up and down every one of my curves. With each roll of my hips, I shuffled forward. When I was close enough, Lark reached out to grab my waist, pulling me down into his lap. I kept the circular motion going, grinding into his erection until he closed his eyes and gasped.

"You wanted to know what makes me so special," I murmured, grabbing his head with both hands to pull his face back from where he had buried it between my breasts. "All I need from you," I whispered, moving more quickly, trying to gauge his receptiveness though his eyes were closed. "Is to tell me where you want me."

It worked. At least, I thought it did. For one triumphant moment, I was straddling the master's son where he lay naked on my metallic table, surrounded by the glare of the lights in my pristine, white killing room. I already had my blade in hand, smiling down at Lark, waiting for the empowering fear I would use to finish the job. It never came. His grey eyes took in his surroundings, traveled the length of steel pointed down at his chest, then closed again while a cry of excitement escaped his lips.

"Oh, sweet girl!" He gasped when his laughter subsided. "We were made for each other."

As I grappled with my shock at his reaction, I felt my control of the Dream waiver. Lark felt it, too, saw the ripple in the appearance of reality and his face changed. I blinked my eyes to find that I was the one on my back, tied by what appeared to be very real black ropes to the corners of the platform in his sitting room. I looked around, trying to get control of my racing heart while figuring out where Lark had disappeared. His voice filled the room though he remained hidden by the shadows.

"This is phenomenal!" he exclaimed, appearing suddenly as a weight across my pelvis though I still could not see him. "Is this the power my father saw in you? It really is amazing!"

"Glad you're enjoying yourself," I snapped, struggling uselessly against my bonds.

Lark fluttered into existence, his grin loosening my bowels. "To think, a slave might experience this kind of power," he reached his hands down to wrap tightly around my throat. I managed to gasp before my airway was forced closed. "It's no wonder you balk when the leash is pulled too tight. If I kill you here, will you die in reality?"

I struggled to nod against the thumb jammed up under my chin. He released me so I could gulp for air. "Better be careful, then," he chuckled, patting my cheek. My frustrated tears could no longer be held in check.

For a while he just played with me. Experimenting with how much control he had over our reality. If he slapped my face, did the skin stay red? If he cracked a rib with his fist, could he heal it with only a thought? I couldn't answer it all. I had never inflicted such damage on a person unless I meant them to die. Would his healing take? I had no idea. I could only hope.

At last, he grew tired. His deliberate need to test my physical limits became more gentle, seductive, as if I had passed his little trial and was therefore worthy of his pleasure. I fought his control where I could. Now and then I would creep towards triumph, sending little rippling vibrations through the air that altered the colour of the sheets beneath me or the curtains surrounding us. It failed every time to save me. My own terror, and the pain he inflicted, destroyed my focus until I was entirely at his mercy. Even when he came inside me, he forced me to join in his climax until the pleasure and the agony became the same sensation.

Afterwards, when I was too exhausted to fight anyway, my bonds fell away and he nuzzled against me as if we were now lovers, enjoying the mere touch of each other. I swallowed the vomit rising to my throat.

Lark pushed himself up, wiping tears from my eyes, tears I hadn't even been aware I was shedding after so long. "You are too good for that old man," his voice dripped with soothing admiration. His eyes, hooded with his own satiated desire, seemed to caress my face with something akin to tenderness. "He doesn't even know about the reality of this place, does he? He has no idea how to truly possess you."

"What do you want?" I managed to whimper, my throat raw from crying out.

"Oh, my silly little creature," Lark crooned, almost sincere with the gentle strokes of his hand over my skin. "I want you to show all this to my father. Particularly that little white room you seemed so fond of."

I squeezed my eyes shut, willing myself to wake up. "You want me to kill Xzan?"

Lark chuckled softly, trailing little kisses across my breasts and up the side of my throat until his mouth found mine. I endured the probe of his tongue with clenched teeth. My renewed resistance amused him. "I want you to kill Xzan," he agreed.

"No," I said. When his eyes widened, I put more force in my voice. "I will not!"

I blinked my eyes and found myself kneeling in an empty room surrounded by darkness. I was still naked, my arms chained to the floor on either side of me so I couldn't stand. A frustrated scream bellowed forth from the pit of my stomach. As the sound faded, a light clicked on, revealing Thomas, hunched over in a set-up mirroring my own. He looked up. When he saw me, restrained against the floor, his muscles strained to break the chains holding him. Before I could cry out a warning, Lark appeared standing over him. In one fluid motion, Thomas' head was pulled back and my knife was pulled across his throat. I fell as far forward as my bonds would allow, screaming until even my own ears stung from the lingering echo. I was just about to give in to my sobs when Thomas appeared again, as he had before. He noticed me once more and struggled to get free. Lark still stood there, this time holding a barbed whip.

"No," I shook my head. "No, please don't."

Lark raised his arm, bringing the whip across Thomas' back with all the force he could muster. I cried out for him to stop until my voice was nothing but a raspy croak and the skin on Thomas' back hung like strips of tattered rags. Blood foamed at his mouth. When he looked up at me one last time, I watched the light in his eyes wink out before he slumped where he sat.

'Do you need to see more?" Lark's voice was now in my ear.

My head was shaking while I watched Thomas' blood continue to pool around him. Lark went on, pressing his body against me and reaching hands around the front as though to arouse my desire. "I could show you more – I can be very inventive, you know – but if we get right down to it the message is the same: you kill my father, or I kill the savage. It is as simple as that."

I felt Lark stiffen behind me, preparing to take me right there, in front of the dead eyes of the first ally I had ever had. A man I dared to admit I might love, somewhere in the deepest chamber of my soul. I felt Lark enter me, thrusting with all the excitement of a vigorous youth, and I stared at my doom before me. I knew I would do as Lark asked. I would kill Xzan. Then I would kill myself, if only to spare me from the fate I knew was waiting for me when all was said and done.

Chapter 16

Lark had it all planned out. He was going to show his father the video of Thomas and I, incite the jealousy he knew to be simmering just below the surface, then Xzan would invite me to his office to punish me for my indiscretion. There I would seduce him, lure him into the Dream, and kill him in the most inconspicuous way I could. It needed to look natural, so Lark would not be suspected. If I fulfilled my duty, Thomas would be sold back to the fighting pits, free at least from the cruelty of Lark Collier if not slavery itself. Me, well, I was resigned to a shortened life, subject to the time when, either in reality or in the Dream, Lark got carried away enough to end my misery. I hoped it wouldn't take too long and I imagined the ways I could speed things along if necessary.

After my time with him, I was sore; I was sure my ribs were bruised if not broken and my voice was gone for a time. Luckily, Lark knew his preferences enough to realize I would need time to recuperate lest his father become suspicious. As if to tease me, I found Thomas free to enter my room the next day. He could sense something was wrong at once.

"Bella?"

I lay on my side on my bed, facing away from him. He didn't touch me, but the weight of his body settled next to me as he sat on the thin mattress. I felt too numb to give in to tears, so I just closed my eyes and pretended to sleep while Thomas tried in vain to coax me into conversation.

"Belladonna," he repeated, as if reminding me I had a name might restore some of my spirit.

"That's not my name," I grumbled at him miserably. "You need to stop calling me that before we both end up flogged." The way his body stiffened on the bed made me glad I could not see the hurt in his eyes.

Thomas would not be deterred. "I know something happened yesterday. I saw Lark leaving your room when I returned. You need to tell me."

Silence. He was waiting for me to tell him the horrid details. Why? So he could judge me again? Shame filled me up, as much for my cruel thoughts as for the memory of being in Lark's Dream. Thomas persisted.

"You must tell Xzan. He may be a heartless bastard most of the time, but he won't stand for it if you've been abused under his roof, even if the wrong-doer *is* his son," Thomas paused and I could hear a measure of reluctant admiration in his voice. "He does have a small measure of honour, I think, though it may be different from others I have met. He may even let me teach the young pup a thing or two." There was amusement in his tone. I might have smiled once, at the image of Thomas tossing Lark around like a newborn babe, but in my mind all I could see was Thomas chained to the floor as Lark dragged my blade across his throat.

After waiting through more silence, Thomas tried again. "I remembered something last night. When I woke here, in the Wilds, that is, there was a small bean plant where I had appeared. It shriveled up right away, but there may be some magic left there. If I can get us back to that place, maybe I can return us to my world. Any ideas how we might get ourselves banished to the Wilds? I promise I wouldn't let any harm come to you out there." A comforting hand settled on my thigh. I flinched, and it was snatched away just as quickly when it felt the strength of my involuntary reaction.

There will be no banishment for me, I wanted to tell him. For me to escape I would need to kill Lark himself. Unfortunately, the penalty for such actions would be much more final than banishment.

Just leave, I wanted to scream at him, except I didn't trust myself not to fall apart the moment I uttered a sound. If I cried, I'd never convince him to leave.

Finally, I felt Thomas stand. He stopped at the door. "I'll not give up on you my glorious Belladonna. Please promise you won't give up on yourself."

When I heard the door close, I curled into a ball and tried to sleep. I welcomed the nightmares. It was easier to relive the horrors Lark imposed on me than risk Thomas finding me vulnerable in our meadow. If he even suspected the extent of the assault, no consequence would be too horrible to stay the hand of vengeance. I knew this without a shred of doubt in my mind.

Now it is I who must protect you my sweet, savage Wilder.

After a particularly vivid nightmare, I found myself dreading sleep at all. I wanted to be held while I wept. I wanted never to be touched again. I saw my grandmother as I had in my dreams, smiling but forever out of reach. I thought of the stories she had told me; I whispered them to myself in the dark:

The Warrior was once a man who walked among us. He fought in many wars and won many battles. Not only was his strength unmatched, his wit and kindness made him a great leader of the people. By his twenty-first year, he was named clan chief of his people and every young man and maiden vied for his affections.

The Warrior was indeed lonely. He often longed for a mate he could walk the world with. His mate would need to be as strong and as kind as he, for he knew the world was a harsh and unforgiving place. He knew he must wait for another soul who could be his equal in all things.

There came a time, after many years of peace and good fortune, when the Warrior decided he must seek beyond his own people. While he was absent, he trusted his people to his brother. Certain that all would be well at home for a time, the Warrior set off at once. They say he travelled to many lands over many more years. He helped the weak to reclaim their lost lands. He fought terrible beasts and saved many lives. Everywhere he went was better for his presence, yet still he felt as if he was but half a man, a part of himself ever empty.

One night, he fell upon his knees and gazed up at the stars in the sky.

"Please," he begged. "Please guide me to the one I am meant to love."

As he watched, a star fell but no answer came to him. He would have risen, defeated, and returned to the village he was staying in, but as he turned to walk away, he found himself facing a great desert cat. It opened its mouth to reveal fangs as long as his forearm and just as thick around. Its roar made the earth beneath the Warrior's feet tremble before it. The Warrior did not tremble. He readied his spear and bellowed back at the beast, for what was one more dance with death when he had bested it so many other times.

Before the cat could take him down, both man and beast became aware of a hiss in the darkness between them. Before either could react to the primal instincts that sounded in their minds, the serpent struck. The desert cat screamed in agony as the snake's venom began to wind its way through its blood. The snake itself slipped away into the night, but the Warrior watched as his adversary slumped to the ground before him.

He did not hesitate. Without fear for himself he knelt at the cat's side and drove the point of his spear against the swelling of the bite on its foreleg. He tried to milk the poisoned blood from the limb by firmly running his hand down it again and again. In the dark, the blood seemed black against the pale sand of the desert. So focused was he on his work, that it took him several minutes to notice that the cat's leg had transformed in his hands. It was no longer thickly muscled or covered in coarse amber fur. It was the smooth, dark skin of a woman's arm. The Warrior looked up in shock.

The woman gazing back at him held his gaze with fierce yellow eyes that bespoke the cat form she had abandoned. "Why did you save me?" she asked, her voice a deep melody. "I had intended for your death, you know."

"I know," he said. "But I am a brave warrior and you a proud huntress. We are not destined to die as prey to lesser beings."

The woman considered him a moment longer before her face broke apart in a broad smile that took the Warrior's breath away. He could see the stars in her smile. "I owe you my life," she said. "How shall I repay this debt?"

The Warrior stood, pulling the woman to her feet alongside him. "Never leave my side," he breathed.

The Huntress' smile faded. "But I am not of this world and cannot stay."

"Then take me with you. I would follow you anywhere."

The woman nodded her head once and together, the couple ascended to the stars. Since that night, the Warrior and the Huntress have never parted. We see their lights burn in the sky and remember the story of how their love began in a single act of selflessness.

As I finished the story in my head, I found myself picturing Thomas in the part of the Warrior. I imagined us floating away together, rising high above Atlantis until its lights could no longer dim the stars overhead. We could take our place among legends of old and never think about the sins and servitude we had endured as part of the world below. The last image in my head before sleep took me was the sight of Atlantis from the safety of the night sky.

Thomas

Thomas struggled to keep the fury inside in check. He had bristled at the sight of Lark Collier leaving Bella's chamber the day before, every one of his instincts telling him something was wrong. When Bella had not met him in the Dream his suspicion became certainty. Now he was sure the young Collier had done something to the woman he had sworn to protect. Frustration drove his fist into the wall. The skin over his knuckles broke open, but the dent he had left in the metal was satisfying.

He couldn't wait for her to ask anymore. He had to get her away from Atlantis before she was killed, or worse. While he paced outside of her room, he almost hoped Lark would show up so Thomas could squeeze the life out of him. His fists clenched at the thought. Yet Thomas knew simple revenge was foolish. It would only get him killed and leave Bella all alone once more. He couldn't do that to her.

While hours passed without notice, Thomas tried to remember the route he had taken with Alder through the Wilds. Granted he wasn't even sure how to get out of the city, but he thought that would be the easy part. Easy compared to escaping the Colliers. And getting across the unforgiving desert? That was a whole different complication. They would need food and water. How many days had it taken back then? His memories had grown fuzzy and the discrepancies in his ability to tell the length of the days when he first arrived in this world confused him. Doubt festered in his mind. He pushed it down in his thoughts. There was no time to doubt. Maybe they would die wandering the Wilds, but at least they would die free.

Plans continued to develop in his mind. He was so focused, the appearance of Red to summon him to Xzan's office made him jump.

"What does that man want now?" Thomas growled. He felt a twinge of guilt at the way Red blanched and scurried away from him, but his frustration had had all day to fester and grow. When he stood outside of Xzan's office, he took a few calming breaths before buzzing himself in.

Xzan stood behind his desk, staring at the pedestals in the corner. His shoulders were tense, hardly moving with each breath he took. Thomas felt his hackles rise at the sight of four other men in the room. They were all fighters to be sure, burly in the Atlantian way if not as big as Thomas. Something was wrong. The metal collar began to itch with the faintest of tingling electric currents.

"You summoned me?" Thomas felt his voice echo back at him. Still, there was no response. He glanced at the other men in the room, trying to discern what their role was, but each had their eyes fixed on a point just in front of their toes. Thomas let his eyes travel back to Xzan. As they did, they passed by the large desk and froze at the sight of the screen hovering just above its surface.

The video was playing on a loop. It must have been, for he did not remember lingering in Bella's arms for so long. She was tall but slender, so it appeared she had been swallowed by his embrace. The peaceful look of desire on her face matched his own and told any who saw it that she was not being forced against her will.

For a second Thomas felt the memory of her lips on his and he fought the urge to smile. Then the second passed and he realized the predicament he was in. What could he say in the face of a man's jealousy that would not see him thrown out of the house? He couldn't abandon her. He opted for silence and waited for Xzan to initiate the punishment.

When Xzan turned it was not jealousy that blazed on his hard features. Though the narrow chin was firmly set, there was no outward emotion at all except torrential rage pouring from the bottomless depths of his eyes. Thomas knew what was coming a moment before it happened.

The electricity charging through the collar seared the skin of Thomas' neck and flung him to the ground. In wild, thrashing motions he alternated between curling into a ball and arching his back into painful contortions as his body fought to expel the excess energy. When it was over, the lingering sensation felt like pins and needles all over his body. His vision was spinning, with patches of black making focus hard to grasp. When the blurriness cleared, Thomas could just make out Xzan standing over him, the remote dangling loosely from long fingers.

"Did you really think I would let the likes of you sully what is mine?" Xzan asked, his voice deceptively calm.

Something inside Thomas snapped. He could no longer contain his rebellion. "She is not yours," he managed, though the words stumbled over his tongue.

Xzan knelt down and grabbed Thomas by the hair. He wrenched the larger man's head until their noses almost touched, and Thomas had *to look directly into Xzan's eyes. "She is mine, more than you will ever know. And you, well, you are a savage hardly worth my morning piss." He let Thomas head go and stood to straighten his robes. "Slaves who presume to take what is not theirs need to be punished."*

Thomas watched Xzan snap his fingers once before four sets of fists pummeled him into oblivion.

Chapter 17

I'm not sure what changed. Perhaps the air in my room had simply grown too stale to breathe. One day I was sulking in a cloak of self-pity, then the next morning I woke-up and I knew the time had come. I dressed in the clothes I had been given to wear to the mayor's party. I grimaced when I remembered the reaction it had garnered from Xzan when he had seen it. It would be perfect. Instead of my usual orderly bun, I brushed my hair off my face and left it to rustle against my back. I fixed my make-up, then stood to stare at myself in the new mirror. Had I changed in the last week? Perhaps my face had always been completely empty of emotion. Whatever fire Thomas thought he saw had been extinguished. I was beautiful. My body appropriately curved, my smooth skin hugging the fine features of my face, but I felt hollow. When the door opened, I turned to leave, walking without real purpose or direction. The stark walls of the corridor led me in the only direction I'd always been walking. Outside Xzan's office, I held my palm against the scanner, wincing when the beep affirmed my ability to enter unannounced.

Xzan sat at his desk, watching the screen in front of him. He didn't even look up from the image of Thomas and me wrapped around each other. His face was empty, his eyes not really seeing the video in front of him. When he spoke, the steadiness of his voice sent a shiver down my spine.

"I suppose it would have happened eventually," he remarked, rising slowly to his feet to face one corner behind his desk. My breath caught when I saw Thomas standing there, strung up by his neck until only the balls of his feet rested on the platform. His hands were tied behind his back and his face was black and blue. "You're all basically animals anyway, no matter how we try to fool ourselves. Lust is a natural thing. I don't blame you."

He finally turned my way and looked at me properly. His eyes lingered on my exposed breasts. "Why do you come to me like this?" His voice was shaking. I had never seen such vulnerability in him before. It was terrifying.

I took a tentative step toward him. "I thought this was what you wanted," I said softly, my eyes downcast while I inched forward. "These clothes were left for me, and my door was opened. I hoped…" I left what I might have hoped unsaid before kneeling before my master.

His hand stroked the top of my head until his fingers caught in a snag in my hair. He fell to his knees before me, tears in his eyes. He turned my chin up, brushing hair from my face. "You are mine." His fingers lost themselves in my hair again, clenching a fistful and yanking until I gasped in pain.

"Yes, master."

Spit flecked against my cheek. "No one else is allowed to have you but me."

"Yes," I sighed, not taking my eyes from his. He hadn't been seduced, but his mind was vulnerable in this state, clouded by anger and his own brand of lust. I could see my opportunity approaching, a door sliding open just behind his eyes. I dared to raise my hand to his face, letting the tears already so close to the surface flow freely. The words came out in a choked plea. "Where do you want me?"

The white room was not as comforting as it had once been. Seeing Xzan stretched out on my table was wrong; he didn't belong there. I let the image slide until he was sitting in a chair, clothed in white robes with hands and feet bound. He didn't seem surprised at all. He looked around, taking in the string of lights hanging from the walls. "If only the room was black," he mused. "We could gaze upon the stars. I know how much you wish to see the stars."

The wishful sincerity of his words made me look around myself. With a single thought, my white room turned black with only the soft glow of my lights to break up the darkness. "Is this what the sky was meant to look like?"

Xzan's face was distorted by shadows. "Yes." I watched him watching me, his eyes taking in the red sweater I preferred to wear in my room. "You look just like your mother."

I schooled my face into rigid indifference. "I will take your word for it. I never met her."

"She was beautiful, even more so when she carried you." Something in his voice triggered a memory I wasn't ready to remember. "You looked just like her the moment you were born. A blessing, really. My wife would not have tolerated you otherwise."

"Why not?" The answer already hung between us.

Xzan cocked his head to the side. He seemed to pity my ignorance. "I never wanted you to know. I feared you would start to want the freedom you could never have. Your grandmother threatened to tell you if I didn't start treating you more like the other slaves. She thought I was setting you up to fail. You wouldn't fit in either of our worlds if you weren't allowed to grow up a part of either." Defeat settled over proud shoulders. He sighed.

I almost didn't recognize the old man in front of me. Xzan Collier was gone.

"She was right, of course. That's why I separated you from the others. She had to go, though. The power you gave her over me was not appropriate. I'm told she lived out her remaining years in relative comfort in Mandar's home. He was always soft with his slaves."

"You said my grandmother had died," I sputtered lamely.

"She has, now, but at the time you were inconsolable. It seemed a kinder thing, to offer you the comfort of death. I hoped it would help you put her from your mind."

You are mine. His words bumped around my head, heavy with unspoken meaning.

"You're my father," I said aloud at last, wondering if I had known it all along. Anger bubbled where regret had been simmering. He maintained eye contact, confirming my accusation with his silence. "That's why you kept me from Lark. That's why you never once demanded of me what you would have me do to those you sent me to."

"I hated sending you to those men, hated myself for caring, but it's how your gift works," Xzan retorted defensively. "If there had been any other way."

"There is," I knelt at his knees. "Did I have to fuck you to bring you here? Men are just easier to manipulate when you dangle sex before their eyes. I've never lain with a man outside of the Dream."

Xzan opened his mouth to refute my claim but stopped. Instead, he nodded. "I believe you." If his hands had been free, I imagine he would have stroked my cheek. I flinched from the imagined touch. "I always longed to call you by the name I picked out for you. Xzya. I feared to give you a part of my name. It would put you at too great a risk."

His tenderness was wrong. Where was the most powerful man in Atlantis? What business did this defeated shell of a man have to bear the name Xzan Collier? I was so full of emotion I struggled to sort out my thoughts. Anger and grief were at the forefront, bursting forth from the knowledge my grandmother had been taken from me and realizing the years we had lost. Beyond that, I found a small kernel of pride stiffening the set of my shoulders.

I smirked as I stood, brushing invisible dirt from my knees. "A name is not a gift you can give or take as you please," I told him, circling around to stand behind the chair. I reached around with one arm, gripping his forehead with my other hand. "It's mine, my reward for enduring the shame of your existence, and I claim it for myself." With a quick jerk, I snapped his neck and stepped back into my body.

Chapter 18

It took me a moment to regain control of my limbs. I hadn't eaten since the morning before, so the dry heaving that kept me on my knees brought nothing up. I looked down at Xzan. He had collapsed in front of me; his eyes were closed, and his face was infuriatingly peaceful. I pushed him over onto his back, checking his heart just to be sure the job was done. If they did an autopsy, they would discover his neck had been broken without a doubt, but it was in Lark's best interest to keep such an investigation from happening. Before calling for help, I dug around in Xzan's clothing. "It's not here," I muttered angrily.

"Bella?"

I leapt to my feet at the sound of Thomas' voice. He was still hanging there, his feet a bloody mess where they struggled to support his weight. "It's not here! The controller for your collar...he doesn't have it," I cried. Outside the Dream, the strength of my emotions gave way to my panic and the trauma of having just murdered the man who had shed the mask of master in his last moments. *My father.*

"Just call for help," Thomas said through gritted teeth. "I'll...be fine."

I nodded, all but throwing myself at Xzan's desk to press the panic button on the underside of the top drawer. The alarm was silent, but it wasn't long before I could hear the thud of approaching footsteps. Before the door could open, I knelt next to Xzan's body; I placed both hands palms-down on my thighs and kept my head tucked so low my chin almost rested on my collar bone. I didn't see who came in first, but Lark's voice was the first to bark orders before the hysterics started.

"Call the physician! Quickly!" I didn't dare look up to see the feigned concern on his face.

Avah Collier came into the room next. She took one look at me, dressed as I was, kneeling next to her husband, and began to pummel me with her fists. She was not a strong woman, but the blows were filled with such fury I felt the bruises forming on my spirit. I made no attempt to block the attack. I didn't see who pulled her from me, but strong hands were soon leading me slowly back towards the corridor to my room. Another body fell in on the other side of me, the crimson tendrils of hair that had escaped her bun telling me it was Red. The door closed on the chaos of the other room behind us. My door was the only other one open, so we headed there. I was finally able to acknowledge whose strong arms had guided me from the chaos left in the wake of my crime. He maintained a stoic silence despite the way he hobbled on sliced feet.

"Lay down," I told him, shoving Thomas onto the bed more easily than should have been possible.

Red set to work immediately, producing a medicinal cream from somewhere on her person to treat Thomas' feet along with the terrible rope burns on his neck. I ran my fingers through his hair, trying to reassure him when the sting of healing caused him to suck in his breath. "I don't know what she is using but it works quickly. It will begin to dull the pain soon. You'll be healed by tomorrow, I swear."

I turned to Red. She had tucked away her salve and was eyeing me strangely. "Thank you, Red, for all the kindnesses you have shown me over the years."

She blinked her eyes. "Red?"

At the sound of her voice, I wanted to laugh and throw my arms around the other woman. I had never once heard her speak. Instead, I settled for a sincere smile. "Everybody should have a name. I didn't know yours."

Red thought about this for a while, looking back and forth between her patient and me. When she smiled, the corners of her eyes crinkled. "I like Red. I will take it."

"Why did you do it?" Thomas seemed to struggle with the question, unsure what could be said in present company. "He was your best protection against Lark."

To buy your freedom, I wanted to say. A life for a life. "He was my father. He told me while we were in the Dream. He sent my grandmother away so she wouldn't tell me the truth."

It was no explanation, but there was some understanding in Thomas' eyes. Let him believe I had murdered my master in a cold rage. It would be better that way. He sat up, ignoring both Red and my attempts to keep him laying down. "We need to get you out of here before things settle down. Lark will not wait for his father's corpse to cool before he takes you again. He probably doesn't know the truth about your relationship."

I opened my mouth to agree when a shadow fell across us from the doorway. At the sight of Lark filling the narrow doorway with a surreal menace, Red fell immediately to her knees. Her submissive conditioning was too strong to ignore. Thomas tried to get up, to block Lark from reaching me, but a sudden convulsion left him spasming on the bed. I cried out, moving to grab his arm when Lark yanked me back by my hair. The collar's controller was held confidently in his hand. "No need to get up, you two. Might as well stay put." I struggled against him to return to Thomas' side. "I'll show this one to her new room myself."

He stepped out of the room, dragging me with him, and locked the door shut on Thomas and Red together. There was nothing more for me to do but go with him, held captive by the grip he maintained on my hair. I hardly paid attention to where we went; the apartment took up three stories and had a maze of halls between each floor. I thought we must be sticking to the slaves' hallways since we passed no one on our journey. At last, we came to a door Lark had to unlock before shoving me inside. Before locking me in, he straightened out his robes.

"I'll be back as soon as I've calmed my mother down. Make yourself presentable."

I lunged at him, my fingers curved as though to claw out his eyes, but I collided with my own reflection in the metal door. I screamed and beat my fists against the barrier keeping me from my target until they bled, smearing red stains over the stainless steel. When the fight had burned out of me, I turned to look at my surroundings properly.

My eyes widened. *When did he do this?*

The room was entirely white, from the walls which still reeked of paint, to the cold linoleum beneath my feet. There was a toilet and sink in one corner where I could clean myself up. The mirror over the sink was bolted to the wall so I couldn't smash it to make a weapon. There was no real bed to be seen, nor any other furniture for that matter, except a cold metal table in the middle of the room. It was too bright. Instead of stringed lights decorating the room, the lights were inset into the walls, making the heat of the small chamber almost unbearable. Between my battery of the door and the excitement of earlier, I was soaked in sweat. My hair clung rudely to my face, and I thought I could smell the odor of my exertions. A rational part of my mind, a part that told me to calm down if I wanted to make a proper plan to escape, made me walk towards the sink to splash water over my face. There was a makeup applicator and a brush on a shelf next to the mirror. A change of clothes waited for me on the floor. I stared at myself in the mirror, steeling my nerves for whatever came next.

The makeup was different. I held the applicator to each eye, startled to see that, instead of the bold eyeliner Xzan preferred, my eyelids had been evenly bronzed and my eyelashes painted to give them an extended, feathery look. There was nothing to tie back my hair, so I settled for brushing it until I felt my frayed nerves patch themselves together. My new clothes were startlingly reserved: a robe, albeit sheer enough to hide absolutely nothing, and a fine silver choker that connected with a matching chain to wear around my waist. Once the robe was on, I could just make out the glitter of the metal beneath the fabric. The robe was long enough to brush against the floor when I started to pace impatiently. With each step, a plan became more fixed in my mind. All I needed now was the courage to see it through.

By the end of the day, I would have freedom or I would have death. I could only hope the two would not greet me as a pair.

Thomas

Thomas watched Bella being dragged away in muted horror. The jolt of current from his collar still stung his already weeping neck, and his limbs no longer wanted to obey him. He was paralyzed.

The door closed and he gave in to his shame. He had failed her. Again. A different woman this time, a different monster, but the failure burrowed itself under his skin until his only release was in the hot tears streaming down his face. His throat ached from the roar of rage that had burst out from his chest before he could truly wallow in his own self-loathing.

A cool hand came to rest against his brow, shocking him out of his stupor. He opened his eyes to find himself staring into the sad face of the red-haired woman. Red. Bella had given her a name.

"She'll be alright," Red assured him, her voice cracked from disuse. "She was born under the stars of the Huntress. She'll not easily allow herself to become prey."

"The Huntress?" Thomas asked. He managed to bring a shaking hand up to wipe the tears from his face.

Red nodded. "The slaves remember the lessons the masters have forgotten. Our ancestors were Wilders themselves, freely roaming the world when the moon was still whole and only one great light filled the heavens in the day. Our grandmothers tell us the stories of their grandmothers, of guardian spirits dominating the sky."

Thomas tried to sit up. "You mean the stars."

Red nodded enthusiastically even as she pushed him back against the mattress. "The corruptions of Atlantis hide them from us now, but my grandmother told me there are pictures of them up there, beyond the gloom." Red paused, then said shyly. "I think perhaps you were born beneath the Warrior's stars."

Thomas imagined a great warrior riding across the sky. He couldn't even remember the last time he had seen the stars. His memory of them had faded into a faint ideal, sparkling lights like sunlight on new armor. He didn't know the stories Red referred to, but maybe there were guardians up there, watching over them. Was it any more insane than considering the shaking of the earth a sign of Nature's displeasure? Was it so different from the God he had known in his own world? Perhaps these guardians were the angels of God. If that were so, then there was still hope. Thomas knew if he ever dared to dream that knighthood could still be his, he must not lose faith. Red hadn't. The older woman seemed so certain; Thomas needed to believe it, too.

Bella would hold her own until he could save her. She was the strongest person he had ever known.

Slowly, the effects of his earlier mistreatment faded along with the paralysis of his electrocution. Thomas' first victory came when he was able to swing his legs over the side of the bed and the world stopped spinning. The medicinal cream had already numbed his feet, beginning the process of knitting shredded skin back together. Still, it took him a long time before he tried to stand. Deep breaths, meant to hone his concentration, also served to settle his nerves. Every precious minute wasted in his recovery was another minute she was with her tormentor. The thought of it drove him to his feet at last, leaning heavily on Red as he adjusted his weight on his tender soles.

Pulling back his shoulders, Thomas stood straighter. He glanced down at the other slave, noted her reassuring confidence, and took one step back towards the back wall. With every ounce of his strength, he let out a fierce cry and charged the door. The metal still shivered as he prepared to charge again.

Chapter 19

I paced the room for what felt like hours. My bare feet slapped painfully against the hard floor until they were too numb to notice anymore. I imagined a hundred ways to kill Lark Collier. I imagined a hundred ways to kill myself if it came to it. None of my imaginings seemed to fit, and I eventually stopped my trek across the room. I was leaning over the metal table, palms pressed firmly down to keep my shoulders from shaking, when I heard the click of the door as its lock disengaged.

The door was not the one I had been brought through earlier. This one had been invisible before it opened in the wall opposite of where I expected. I stood straighter but did not move towards the only exit I had available to me at that moment. I waited for Lark to step through. I waited and considered not leaving my room at all, however no one entered my space and I wanted to be done with this. The length of a steadying breath was the last testament to my earlier hesitation before I walked towards whatever came next.

I didn't have far to go. The door to my new room opened directly into Lark's private sitting room. He had changed it since I had been there last. The curtains on the middle platform had been pulled back and the cushions replaced with what appeared to be a thick red blanket draped over its hard edges. I tried not to notice a tangle of ropes hanging from above, some already looped in a way I knew from the Dream was meant to bind me to the will of my master. *I have no master,* I told myself, over and over again in my mind. My master was dead. I had killed him. I would never let the man who Dreamed up the display I was looking at take ownership of me.

The man in question watched my appraisal of his handiwork with some curiosity. He had been laying on his side. As I came closer, he sat up, heedless of the way his open robe revealed an underwhelming lack of interest in my appearance. The prospect of what it might take to arouse him made me sick, but I would not let him see it. I schooled my features into a display of calm indifference in the face of his dark smile.

"You did well," he praised, raising a glass he had been cradling in one hand before finishing off its contents. "How did you do it?"

"I broke his neck," I said. I began to circle around the pedestal, keeping several paces out of reach. His eyes followed me.

"Did you have to seduce him first?"

Inside I cringed at the way he rubbed at himself as he asked his questions. Aloud I only said: "No. He trusted me, and so my way into his mind was open." There was a small twinge of guilt when I realized my words rang with truth. My anger no longer burned hot enough to keep it at bay.

Lark didn't bother to hide his disappointment. He stepped down from his pleasure stage and fetched himself another drink. "I guess it doesn't matter. What's done is done. Once I got my mother properly sedated, it was easy enough to get the examiner to rule it a heart attack. No investigation, no hiccups in the inheritance. Well, almost no hiccups. It's a minor thing, one I may very well remedy tonight."

I kept putting one foot before the other. "What might that be?"

Lark's smile faltered when he narrowed his eyes at me. "You see, there you go, forgetting your place again." His smile returned and he turned to lean casually back against the bar. "Maybe you enjoyed my lesson the other night. Is that it? Ready to go another round?"

"Are you?" I was relieved to hear my voice did not tremble as easily as my legs did. "The Dream is mine. I am the master there. You may not be so lucky this time."

Lark pushed himself away from the bar to take a step towards me. "Maybe it was you who was lucky until now. You may have inherited the genetic jackpot, but in this case second prize might just be good enough for me. I may need you to get there, but we both know who is the master and who is the slave in your Dream."

There it was in the open. I knew now without a doubt: he knew the truth about us. Perhaps his mother had mentioned it. Perhaps his father had, though I doubted it. Or maybe... "The will," I gasped when realization set in. "He recognized me in the will, didn't he?"

The violence with which Lark swung his arm to smash his glass against the wall behind my head was all the confirmation I needed. "He was *my* father! Don't you dare sully our name by claiming such a place in his heart."

"What, did he leave me your share of the apartment?" I sneered, finding courage in his lack of control. "If that's the case I'd like to thank you for painting my bedroom for me. It's just the way I like it."

Lark was on me in an instant, throwing me backwards with every ounce of his strength. In the real world my own strength counted for little, but the couch broke my fall nicely. I was soon back on my feet, facing him eye to eye. "So, what was it? What did he leave his bastard slave that has you so scared?"

We were standing close enough for me to feel his breath on my face. "Your freedom," he growled.

His answer left me frozen in place. *Freedom.* The concept, once so alien to me, dangled within my grasp. *I am free?*

Xzan had said I was his. Only his. Here he was, dead, and I feared the line of succession would put me at the mercy of a true monster. But I would never belong to another. Never again.

"I'm free," I gasped, the words settling a sense of giddy excitement over me. It was a mistake to indulge it.

Lark seized the moment. Before I could gather my wits, he had pinned me to the couch, both of his hands wrapped firmly around my throat. I could see now the hiccup he meant to deal with. He had never meant for me to survive this next encounter; he was just cocky enough to hope for a little more fun before he gave up his new toy.

Not this time.

I forced myself to concentrate on meeting his eyes instead of fighting for breath. Even as my field of vision narrowed to hardly more than Lark's face, I fought to penetrate the icy grey of his eyes. I saw him lose his control, his hold on reality, and I struck with the swiftness of a falling star.

The world reversed itself so fast neither one of us was fully prepared. I recovered first, creating my place in the Dream with such force there would be no undermining my authority. We were in my white room, Lark laid out on my table, my knife raised above my head. He struggled against his bonds, trying to shout around a gag of air I had formed in his mouth.

"I would love to show you the pleasures you showed me, big brother, but frankly, I just don't have the time." His eyes bulged in his face the moment my knife pierced his chest. Blood bubbled around the blade, oddly dark before it spread a red satin sash over his pecs and shoulders. Even with his lifeblood spilling to the floor, those eyes glared sullenly at me. It was as if his rage had taken on enough life to save him for a time. I twisted the knife until I felt it grate against bone and it became lodged between two ribs. The fight drained out of the man beneath me, pooling on the floor in one bright puddle. I waited until the light in his eyes died, until I was sure no breath rose in his chest. Then I let the Dream slip away.

Chapter 20

I left Lark in his entertaining room. There was a door from there to his bedroom. It was difficult not to spend too much time in there. It wasn't as though Lark had been overly flamboyant in his choices of colour or variety, nearly every garment was black or grey, but I still felt swollen with the power of the Dream and such mastery swept away all vulnerability.

I was free. Maybe not for long and maybe only because I had murdered my master, yet in that moment, in the real world, I was free.

The powers that be would probably toss me in Dungeon and throw away the keys if they found out my role in Xzan's plots. Besides, considering the way I had left my brother lifeless in the other room, I'd be lucky not to be put to death on the spot.

I fingered the soft fabrics of Lark's clothes with the hesitant desire of a virgin caressing the object of her desire. I wanted to throw every shred of it away. I wanted to wear it all. In the end, reality returned and along with it, caution. There were two dead Colliers now; both killed by my hand. Even if they never linked me to Xzan, there was no denying I had been the last one with Lark. Surely his room had as many cameras as Xzan's had had. His exam would show significant internal bleeding, and even with no apparent wound, Avah Collier would not rest until I had been punished. It was time to leave.

I dressed in black leggings and a red shirt I took from Lark's wardrobe. I spared a moment to speculate on our similar tastes as I took in my appearance in. Lark was fortunately not much larger than I, so the leggings were suitably snug around my hips if a little long, and the tunic hung suggestively off one shoulder. The boots I pulled on were a bit too big too. After I was satisfied with my own appearance, I found what I could for Thomas. My searching grew reckless, clothes tossed over my shoulders while I worried over how even the bulkiest robe would be too small. While I rooted around the wardrobe, I also found the remote control for Thomas' collar. It had been hidden in a drawer with an old switchblade. I took both, wondering if I would be able to use such a blade in real life.

Slipping back into Lark's room made me stop to consider what I was doing. His body, still sprawled awkwardly on the couch, caught my attention. I couldn't remove the collar without the owner's fingerprints. I reasoned Lark had probably already gone through the process of switching ownership in the apartment database. It might even be automatic. I could only hope. It was hardly more than a click of a button after all. What power could he have truly had over me without also having power over Thomas? It may even be how Lark found out about the will so quickly. Before I could really think about what I was about to do, I took the switchblade from my bundle and set to work.

Real life is much messier than the Dream.

Carrying Lark's finger made the rest of my journey somewhat easier. At first, I didn't know how to get back to my old rooms. The apartment seemed empty, with only a few slaves going about their business while their masters presumably slept away their grief. I avoided these men and women completely. At last, I found the entrance to Xzan's office. Lark's finger gained me access in an instant. The room was no longer so imposing now that its owner was lying dead in a morgue somewhere. I moved through it to the slave's entrance without a second glance at the torturous pedestals behind the desk. I would never stand on them again.

The empty corridor felt longer than usual, though. Pausing outside of my door, I feared what opening it might reveal. It had felt as though Lark had left me waiting for a lifetime. I couldn't imagining how Lark had used that time, and who he might have hurt while I waited for his attention. Sucking in a deep breath, I held the bloody finger to the scanner, stepping back when the door opened to brace myself for what I might find.

It was a good thing I had.

As soon as the door had finished sliding into itself, Thomas flew into the opposite wall, the momentum of his body leaving him off balance. Red was the first to see it was me waiting off to one side. Relief pulled back the corners of her lips. That is, until she saw what I was wearing, and what I was holding in one hand. The smile was quick to fade.

"We must get you out of here," she said.

Thomas, having recovered from his offensive attack, took me in his arms to swing me around as much as the narrow hall would allow. My treasures scattered on the floor. "How?"

I shrugged. "It turns out I'm a free woman. I was released from my bond in Xzan's will."

Thomas raised a tawny brow. "And Lark just let you go?"

I bent to retrieve the important appendage I had dropped. I twirled it around between us. "He needed some convincing. I can't say he took the news well."

Thomas took the finger from me, scowling at it with unreadable eyes. Whether he was impressed or not didn't show, not even for the most fleeting of moments. He met my expectant gaze, his lips moving as though to speak, but nothing came out. Just as anger was beginning to cloak my pride with resentment, Thomas pulled me against his chest in a hug fit to crack my still sore ribs.

"You're welcome," I gasped, tears stinging my eyes. I tried to laugh. "But if I have to save you in the future, try not to break me in half when you express your gratitude."

"Daft, stupid woman," his lyrical voice was filled with so much emotion I couldn't tell if he meant to insult me or burst into relieved tears. "I thought I told you I'd be doing the saving from now on."

"It wouldn't be as interesting if I couldn't take care of myself," I countered. "What kind of 'beautiful death' would I be if I couldn't kill a man?"

"You'll be the death of me if I have to endure such fear again," Thomas replied with such severity I was taken aback. He tried to soften the edge of his voice. "I have never felt so powerless in my life. I didn't know if I would see you again." One rough hand pushed a lock of hair from my face. I leaned into the gesture, appreciating the sensation of his palm scraping against my skin.

The moment ended with an abrupt clearing of Red's throat. When we looked over at her, the fear creasing her forehead had added years to her appearance. "You must get away from here."

I quickly remembered the danger we were in. Lark had claimed his mother was heavily sedated, but a slave might discover the young master's remains at any moment. I couldn't count on any of the others to be as open to rebellion as Red had proven to be.

I removed the collar from Thomas' neck, tossing it, along with the controller, into my room. It clattered against the metal frame of the bed making each of us jump. Thomas dressed in the clothes I brought him, having to settle on the sandals he already had since no boots I found would fit him. Even the robe could barely be tied closed over his broad chest. His calves were more than half bared where he surpassed Lark in height. Red helped us both adjust our clothes until as much of our person was covered as possible.

"Only slaves reveal their skin," she reminded us. There was a distinct pride in her voice as she arranged the oversized sweater over my head like a cowl that might shadow my face while still sheltering my torso from prying eyes. "You are no longer slaves."

By the time she was finished, we could pass for a lower-class woman and her manservant. It would have to do, and if such assumptions were made, Thomas' lack of coverage could be overlooked.

We followed Red down into the kitchens, waiting just outside while she packed us a small satchel of food. The little ENSA cubes would see us through a couple weeks if we rationed with care. She also gave us each a large bottle of water to tie at our waists. The whole time we waited, twitching from one foot to another, I struggled to come up with the words to thank her, to beg her to come with us. In the end, standing in the family's elevator, no words were necessary. Red smiled and dipped her head once in a show of respect. Then she closed the door on any good-byes I might have said.

Chapter 21

I had never imagined trying to leave the city for the Wilds, but I didn't think it would be difficult. There were few guards along the outer walls of Atlantis. Even slaves were not considered stupid enough to take their chances in such a wasteland, where there was no water to be had and little in the way of food. However, we were not so sure of ourselves to risk the main gates. I was sure it would not be long before the authorities were notified of Lark's murder. Then the hunt for us would begin. I knew we needed to be free of the city by the time that happened.

I had never tried to traverse the city on foot before. Every time I had left the apartments, I had been in a vehicle. Still, I had some notion of direction to guide us. Fate lent a generous hand as well. The first glow of daylight had turned the ebony night into a murky grey, illuminating the path we should take. Our blessing was also our curse, for the shadows to which we tried to keep were less numerous the longer we travelled. Every time a vehicle passed by, we shrank away. So far none had borne the black shield or flashing lights of an Authority officer, but my nerves were becoming more frayed with every passing moment.

Atlantis was a labyrinth of glittering towers and ill-kept roadways. The progression of the dawn was slow, yet I began to panic as I felt the hours stretch out, and still there was no sign of the wall. The towers were giving away to smaller apartments. This was a promising sign that we were close, and we could now see the wall towering above the buildings, but I had broken out in a terrified sweat in an effort not to run blindly in any random direction. Roads and alleys had a tendency to circle back on each other or veer in a new direction without warning. The solid presence of Thomas at my side offered some reassurance, but his bulk was attracting unwanted attention from the few people we passed in the street.

We stopped at the sound of a siren wailing overhead.

My eyes darted up the corner of the nearest building, straight into the reflective gaze of a camera pointed right at us.

"Shit!" I cursed, grabbing Thomas hand before walking forward again. It took everything I had to keep my pace to something resembling a casual walk. "How could I forget about cameras in the street?!" It seemed so obvious now. Surveillance was a natural part of our home, a nuisance I had little reason to notice; until recently, that is.

"Why would there be cameras in the streets?" Thomas pointed out, trying his best to hunch his shoulders and appear as small as he could.

"People's safety is the usual excuse," I growled under my breath. My frustration was heightened by my own habitual obedience while under surveillance. It occurred to me that a free woman wouldn't watch the ground at her feet with such ferocity. Some habits are hard to break.

The sirens were beginning to thrum inside my head when the wall appeared down an alley to our left. I wanted to let out a whoop of excitement. I thought I heard the pound of booted feet somewhere behind us but there was no time to look back. Freedom. I had it in my grasp and I would never let go of it again.

"There!"

Thomas' abrupt shout brought my attention to a drainage pipe creating a dark portal through the steel panels of the wall. Iron bars, thick with slime, were all that stood between us and the putrid smell of our path to freedom. Thomas charged ahead of me, gripping the bars in his hands. His teeth were bared, though they couldn't hold back the roar of his efforts. The cover broke free of ill-kept, rusted bolts and crashed to the ground at our feet. We both swung our heads to see if the crash would bring anyone running our direction. The voice of a man barking orders was barely audible, but it spurred us on nonetheless.

Thomas was panting heavily when he turned to offer me his hand. "Let's get the hell out of here."

Somehow, I found the courage to smile. Taking his hand, we let the dark pipe swallow us.

Chapter 22

We followed wisps of fresh air through the putrid stench of sewage. Darkness was all there was for what felt like hours. Thomas led the way, my hand clutched painfully in his. He was almost bent in half to keep his head from hitting the top of the pipe. I was fairing only a little better; my height was enough that soon my own back ached from the way I hunched over myself. The pipe felt as though it must turn, or at least cut diagonally through the wall, for I could not fathom it being so thick as to swallow us in darkness. The very thought of the weight of metal and concrete above our heads already felt suffocating. What if we had simply exchanged one labyrinth for another? All we could do was take one step after another and pray we had not escaped Dungeon for a prison of another kind.

There was no sound of pursuit behind us, though if any had come across the grate we had left tossed on the ground there would be no doubt how we had made our escape. Slowly, the smell of waste lost a measure of its power over the subtle fresh air at the end of the tunnel. My hand, which had been sliding along the wall of the tunnel on my left, found itself in open air and I stumbled. I turned my head to see an opening in the tunnel, and the promising light of dawn beyond its grate. Thomas saw it, too. The rusted bolts were in as poor shape as the last grate, so the two of us were able to use our weight to shove it free. It thudded against the ground where it fell, sending up a cloud of dust to welcome us into the Wilds.

The night was finally coming to an end. A new sunrise waited for us along the horizon of a barren land that stretched out in every direction as far as the eye could see. It was tragically beautiful after the hideous dank life we now left behind. There was a commotion over our heads, from the top of the wall. With our backs pressed against it, we both looked up. From such a distance, we couldn't make out what I feared were armoured officers watching for signs we had made it through.

"What should we do?" I ask.

Thomas' brow furrowed, the dirt in the creases of his forehead standing out like lines drawn in sand. "What kind of weapons might they have? Anything that can kill us from a distance?"

I thought hard. I knew officers carried tasers and clubs on their person, but I had never heard of a long-range weapon. I told Thomas this, then added, "But I have hardly had reason to find out if I'm right or not."

Thomas gripped my hand even harder. "Well, then I guess we'll make a run for it and hope for the best. You ready?"

I nodded.

Alpha was climbing slowly over the horizon. The light from our largest sun illuminated the thin line of dust we created as we raced for cover in a nearby outcrop of rocks. I risked several glances over my shoulder, certain our trail would be marked by the watchmen on the wall. If they could see our flight, they were likely already sending officers to march from the nearest gate.

The thought made my worn-out muscles carry me faster. *At least the cars don't work outside the city.* This gave us little advantage, though. We were both tired and hungry, and Thomas' sandals couldn't protect where his feet had hardly had the chance to heal. Fresher men would catch us in no time.

The small cluster of rocks protruded from the ground like grasping fingers a mile from the wall. It was there our legs gave out and we collapsed at last. Resting in the cool shade, checking over our shoulder for signs of pursuit, we finally let out a collective breath of relief.

"We made it!" I exclaimed with a bright smile on my face.

"For now," Thomas agreed, leaning his head back against the rock. His face revealed nothing. "Will they follow us out here? Or just leave us to die?"

I looked back over the rocks, my eyes narrowed. I could just make out a small entryway in the wall but no movement. There was no cloud of dust to mark where others disturbed the earth in their pursuit. "If they saw us, they probably think we have sent ourselves to our own death. Avah won't be satisfied by this, but it might take her some time to makes someone's life miserable enough to bother with a couple of suicidal runaways."

Thomas laughed. "Let's hope the search is half-hearted at best. You've set them free of a tyrant, I think. They will hardly bend to Mrs. Collier the way they did to her husband."

I fervently hoped so.

"So, my fine, otherworldly Wilder, where is your portal home?" I teased, shoving my elbow into his ribs. I was too elated by this sudden freedom to rest in the shadow of Atlantis for long.

Thomas turned to me and smiled. Raising one hand, he pointed toward the first of the two suns rising slowly in the North. "That way."

My eyes followed where his finger had pointed, shielding my eyes from the brightness of the new day. It seemed as though there was nothing ahead of us, not even a boulder for shade, once we gave up our current shelter.

"How do you know?" I asked. "You said it's been fifteen years." I swallowed a lump in my throat, praying we would not be walking towards our doom. *Better to die free,* I reminded myself. It had become my mantra in recent days it seemed.

Thomas stood and brushed sand from his clothes before offering me his hand. "You're right, it has been a while. I could even be wrong, but I do remember the way the suns moved across the sky, their strangeness I will never forget, and I have a good feeling." He paused when he saw the look of doubt in my eyes. He brought a hand up to cup my chin and our eyes met. "You've reminded me what it means to have faith in something. I hope you have faith in me too."

I nodded. "Alright then. Lead on"

Thomas smiled. "We'd best hurry along while it's still cool. Avah Collier may not have the clout her husband did, but like you said, she doesn't seem like a lady who would let someone escape justice. If my memory serves, once both of those suns are up we won't want to keep walking – let alone run – for very long."

My hand went instinctively to the full water bottle I carried. "I hope we reach your bean plant before Omega joins us. We will not last long in the full heat of the day."

Thomas could not agree more, so before the second sun could add its brilliance to the heat of Wilds, we started out again. We moved as quickly as we could while the air held on to the chill of the night, but dust choked our chests and rocks cut through our shoes, shredding the soles of our feet. Still, we were free. We told ourselves we could go on forever with such hope in our hearts. It was pure foolishness of course. As both suns took their places in the sky, it turned out freedom was a hard hope to hold onto. The temperature rose and the reality that night was still weeks away began to gnaw at my thoughts. We slept once, but only when exhaustion drove us to our knees in the scorching heat, and it was short. There were no clocks to tells us whether we walked for hours or for days. Neither sun seemed to move much, though Omega moved enough to nearly overtake her larger sky-mate. I shuddered when I realized this likely meant at least forty-eight hours had passed since we left the city of Atlantis behind.

Once, we happened upon a great boulder jutting out of the earth at an awkward angle. It gave us some relief from the suns. Its appearance also seemed to bolster Thomas' resolve that we were moving in the right direction. I had started wondering if we may still be in Atlantis after all, executed for our crimes while our souls were doomed to wander the hellish afterlife we deserved.

"I remember this rock," Thomas panted between gulps of sun-soaked air.

"How much further?" my voice felt as though it would scrape the inside of my throat raw.

Thomas squinted his eyes to the North as if he could see our destination. "I don't know. I can't tell the passing of time any better now than I could then."

I closed my eyes, too dehydrated to give in to my tears of frustration. "Were the suns up or down?"

Thomas shifted next to me. "When I woke the first time there were two. By the time we reached Atlantis, only one remained in the sky just above that horizon." I opened my eyes to squint westward.

"Must have been several days then," I groaned, trying to calculate the passage of hours without the time pieces I was used to. "We aren't going to make it much further with only a few gulps of water between us." I shook the almost empty bottles we had brought. "Food we have plenty of, water is more important."

"Aye," Thomas agreed, scratching at the new growth of what was quickly turning into a beard. "I know we passed some water along the way. I think it was an old well. I don't know how far."

"What's a well?"

"A hole in the ground filled with water. I remember because Alder made me haul the bucket up."

"Hmmm," I closed my eyes again, picturing an oversized boy pulling water from the ground.

I don't know at what point the daydream became a true dream.

The boy threw his bucket back into the ground, watching as it was swallowed by darkness. Then he looked up at me. I was standing just across from him, wearing the sheer gown Lark had made me dress in for his amusement. The tawny haired youth in front of me held out his hand to reveal three tiny stones shaped like kidneys nestled against his dirty palms.

"We've been waiting for you," he smiled, though the curve of his lips did nothing to lessen the wary look in his haunted green eyes.

"We-?"

"These are for you." The boy twitched the offered hand to draw my attention back to it. When I reached out my own hand, he poured the stones onto my palm. I could feel the thrum of life resonating in them. Their pink skins began to glow in pale imitation of the suns beating down on our heads. I looked back up at the boy for guidance.

"Throw them in," he told me, his lyrical voice floating to me as if only a distant echo. He gestured to the well with a nod of his chin.

The stones danced around in my hand with eager anticipation. Throw us in, they begged me. I obliged.

At first there was nothing. I watched the black pit swallow the beautiful stones as it had done the boy's bucket. After long moments of deadened silence, I looked back up at the boy. He was smiling broadly, hands clenched at his sides.

The ground shook.

I watched as anticipation turned to horror. The boy looked up at me, uncertainty and confusion on his face as plain as the growing whites of his eyes. It took me a moment to realize he was only mirroring what must certainly be my own expression. The violence of the earth's tremor brought me to my knees. I clutched at the hard ground beneath me as if to hold myself in place. Ripples spread from around the well, tossing us both back to the ground. Then came the roar. The boy shouted at me, but I could not hear him over the sound of it. Water shot out of the well into the sky like a pillar of glass glittering in the suns. I felt something cool against my feet and looked down to see water was pooling all around me now, turning the dry earth into thick sludge. Still the ground shook. Terrified, I looked for the boy. He was gone. His voice, penetrating the chaos at last, called out to me.

"Bella, get up! Bella, run!"

Chapter 23

"Belladonna!"

I came back to myself slowly, the Dream still holding me fiercely in its grip. Someone was clutching my arm, dragging me along the ground. Or shaking me. Both? It felt as though I had sand beneath my eyelids. Only when I finally got them open did I realize there was sand in the air around us. Even squinting I could barely make out Thomas, desperately trying to drag me along a ground that heaved beneath his feet. Finally startled enough to scramble to my feet, I opened my mouth to cry out, only to choke on the sand-soaked air. If I had thought we were in hell before, I was sure of it now. Together, Thomas and I held each other to keep from being pitched to the ground while clouds of dust rose from the restless earth. I squeezed my eyes shut, pressing my face against Thomas' chest in an effort to find clean air to breathe. While the entire world seemed to explode around us, I took comfort in the sweet musk of male sweat.

When it stopped, everything fell eerily silent.

Not even my heart dared to resume galloping in my chest.

Thomas was the first to speak, his voice scraping against a dry throat. "There you go, scaring me to death again."

I heard the attempt at a smile in his voice, but when I dared to peek from where I had buried my face in his chest, the sight of the rock we had just sought shelter beneath lying flat on its side made me tremble. We had almost been stuck there, crushed because we dared to seek shelter from the suns. The great giant appeared to have broken right at the base, like a giant had come down and sliced it with a great knife. I stepped away from Thomas to look properly, raising a hand to my eyes to protect them from the dust still hanging in the air. The leftover slab of rock that remained nestled in the earth was perfectly round, with veins of white slithering here and there like serpents.

"Reminds me of Arthur's table," Thomas spoke as he joined me. "Smooth and round like that." He shook his head to dislodge the dirt from his hair then looked at the stone more closely. His forehead wrinkled in concentration. "Actually..."

"What?" I asked him.

"It looks exactly the same," He knelt to trace a grubby finger along one of the white veins where it swirled back into itself before crossing two more of its brethren. "I only saw the round table once, mind you, but this here, I remember this."

"Perhaps you misremember," I suggested glancing around us, surprised to see how normal everything still looked besides the boulder. I had half expected to see the earth rippling out like sheets after a restless night in bed. "It's been many years, after all"

Thomas sighed. "You're probably right," he agreed. "Couldn't possibly be the same stone."

"We need to get to the well," I told him. I took his hand to get him moving. My feet were tingling with the need to run. "I think the things we are searching for are there."

Thomas looked hard at me. "You were in the Dream. That's why I couldn't wake you."

I nodded. "I didn't mean to be. You were there, though, as a boy." I hesitated. *We have been waiting for you.* The boy had said we...I shook the thought from my head. "We were at the well and you handed me three little stones. I think I was about to get a good look at your beanstalk before the earthquake interrupted the connection."

"We'd better move, then." Thomas moved ahead of me. "We haven't much water left, and the suns will only get hotter."

We travelled on in silence. The earth shivered now and then beneath our feet, but nothing like the rolling distress it had unleashed on us before. We didn't stop either. At least, not until heat and exhaustion beat us to the ground. I began to imagine days passing by unaware. Our rations were still strong, being what they were, but our water eventually ran out. When this happened, there was no more stopping. Our lives depended on moving forward.

I began to wonder at Thomas' strength. He drank less than me, and carried me when I needed to rest, yet still each of his steps came as sure as the next. There was no doubt in my mind that he was not from this world. No Atlantian or Wilder had ever been built as strong as him, in body or spirit. I began to resent my weakness. A lifetime of gentle servitude had not prepared my body for this kind of abuse. While my mind remained sharp, aware of my task and certain of the path we were treading, my body betrayed me; I stumbled more and more frequently.

Thomas always picked me back up, and we would go a little further.

I estimated it was the fourth or fifth day when even Thomas' strength gave out. He fell to his knees before me, licking cracked, bleeding lips with a dry tongue. The sun had burned us both beyond the colour of Red's hair. *Red.* Oh, how I longed for her salve at the sight of the weeping blisters on my companion's bared shoulders. I must have looked just as bad, though I imagined his fairer skin might be more vulnerable than my own.

Kneeling beside him, I lay a hand on his arm. "We have to keep moving," I told him, my voice a raspy whisper.

Thomas only shook his head. "I've failed you, my lady. We are going to die out here because I made you follow a dream."

"Hey, now. I'm the mistress of Dreams, remember? I know their power better than you."

A small smile brought beads of blood and pus to his lips. "Can you forgive me?"

"No," I replied. "I will die on the march before I die on my knees. Thanks to you, I will never kneel again, not even to death."

I rose with great difficulty, lurching towards a pile of stones just ahead of us. I tripped over one, catching myself clumsily against its fellows. With a start, I realized I was staring into a black hole in the earth. It was only my hands on the pile of rocks that stopped me from falling in head-first. Moving only my eyes, I regarded the stones nearby. Toppled over as they were, they still formed a perfect circle around the hole. On the far side, I saw the rope. With a whoop of strangled joy, I scrambled around to it. We had made it! It hurt to clamp my hands around the lifeline before me. The coarse fibers set my skin on fire where they left tiny slivers in my palms. It took every ounce of weary strength I had, but I soon had a sloshing bucket of murky water coming up to meet me. When I had set it on the ground, I almost pressed my entire face into it before I remembered Thomas.

He remained kneeling where I had left him, only a few feet away, his head hanging towards his chest.

"Thomas!" I cried, spilling more water than I would have liked while I stumbled back to him. "We made it. Look!"

I placed the bucket before him. He didn't move at first and my heart dropped. Just as I was about to shake him, I saw his hand reach towards the rim of the bucket. It dipped into the water, bringing precious little to his lips. After the first tentative sip, he looked up at me. He was smiling in earnest. "It hasn't spoiled."

"Drink," I told him, somehow finding the tears to cry.

"You first, my lady, but slowly," he warned. "Or you'll be sick."

I nodded. I cupped both my hands together and dipped them into the water. It was blissfully cold. When I had had several such handfuls, and my throat no longer burned with the desire for more, I sat back from the bucket to give Thomas leave to drink. He must have forgotten his own advice. He lifted the bucket and poured what was left over his face while taking whatever tremendous gulps he could. Drops of water clung to the hair on his face and chest, sparkling in the sunlight. I laughed, heedless of the way the skin on my lips split open. I had found beauty in the Wilds at last.

Thomas refilled the bucket for us until we were thoroughly satisfied. We quenched our thirst, soaked our clothes, and cleaned the wounds on our feet. All that was left was to fill our water bottles. While Thomas worked on this task, I began to explore the rubble more closely.

The only sign of human use was a single collar half hidden by dirt. The elements had made it no more than a useless relic; I believed it had been years since the Slavers had come this way. I knew they didn't leave the city at all anymore, but I could not recall exactly when that had become true. We had come so far and seen not one other living soul. Not a Wilder, not a terrifying beast. Not even a stubborn shrub dared to live under the harsh scrutiny of the suns. The only birds I had seen had been within sight of the city. What was left out here?

Maybe this was the reason for the new laws they were trying to pass in Atlantis. If there were no Wilders left, if there were only Atlantians to prey on, someone had to have the power to control a waning economy. I thought I understood the desire to cling to a dying way of life, but it made me angry none-the-less. The collar teased me where it stuck out of the earth. It didn't belong there, but it had embedded itself anyway. I kicked it with all my might, sending it clattering away across the packed clay.

Where it had been there was now a dark gouge in the earth where the sun would soon suck the life from. I knelt to examine the rich red dirt where moisture still seemed to cling. My hand hovered over it in a pitiful attempt to preserve the rich red as long as I could, when I noticed something else. Something green.

A living thing had tried to find a way to survive in what shelter the collar had provided. A fragile stem sprouted from the ground with a single teardrop leaf leaning over one side. I brushed my finger against it, marveling at the soft sign of life before me. I bent lower to get a closer look, my still wet hair dripping into the dirt around it. It must have been as thirsty as we were. As a droplet from my hair touched the ground the plant shivered with delight. Before my eyes the stem grew a little longer and a second leaf unfurled just below the first.

"Thomas!" I cried, my eyes not daring to look away. "You need to see this."

Thomas was at my side in an instant, sharing in my amazement. "It's a bean plant."

His voice was so certain I took him at his word. "Watch this," I told him, bringing forward some of my hair to squeeze more water onto the grateful green thing.

Once again, the little bean plant showed its gratitude by reaching just a little higher towards our eager faces. A third leaf unfurled, and I began to see the fine ridges on the other two as they widened. Thomas sucked in a breath. He had our water bottles with him, so he poured a generous amount on the burgeoning plant. It responded at once. In seconds, it was as long as my forearm. The leaves were like soft green boats curled up slightly at the edges to reveal tiny ribs beneath. Flowers bloomed only to shed their delicate petals while two pods elongated and took form. The pods weighed down the plant, reversing its skyward climb until the vine had tumbled to its side. Once it had hit the dirt, there it remained, somehow sadder and more neglected than it had been before ever it tasted the water we offered.

I smiled broadly at my companion, astounded by such magic appearing before my eyes. Thomas uttered a curse I had never heard before in all my dealings with the underbelly of Atlantis.

"What's wrong?"

Thomas stood to kick the ground with enough force to send a thick layer of dirt over the fallen plant. I was quick to brush it off, plucking the heavy pods in an effort to help the plant regain some of its proud height. "This isn't how it happened last time," Thomas growled. The muscles in his jaw clenched on more angry words.

I looked down at the pods in my hands. Delicate white veins braided their way around each seam. I handed one of the pods to Thomas. "In the Dream, you gave me little stones to toss into the well. Perhaps this is what the magic intended for you to have."

Thomas regarded the pod I had placed in his hand. A smile tugged at the corner of his lip as he began to shake his head again. "You're right, of course. It was the beans that brought me here. It will be the beans that take me home again."

I resisted the urge to laugh at him. "I never realized before what a temper you Wilders have."

Thomas may have blushed beneath the deep burns on his face and he had the grace to laugh at himself. "Aye, I'm sure I have one, alright. I reckon my temper is what landed me here in the first place."

I closed a hand over the fist in which he held the pod. "Then let's see if we can get away from here."

Thomas nodded. Carefully, he peeled away the sides of the pod to reveal the perfect kidney-shaped stones within. They were exactly as I remembered them, pink and covered in silvery threads. Thomas had called them beans. Perhaps that was what they were, but I thought they were more beautiful than any precious gem I had ever seen before. Thomas' eyes, when they met mine again, were wide with unshed tears. "I'm afraid," he confessed, his voice cracked from more than the sun. "I'm afraid I will toss these into the well, but nothing will happen. What if the magic only works once?"

I thought about it, about the boy-Thomas handing me the beans in the Dream. I said nothing, though, because Thomas had already held the beans out for me to take back. I tucked the other pod away in the bag I carried so I could cradle the beautiful beans in both hands. I could already sense the life in them. They hummed against my skin, spreading cool warmth up my arm until my whole body tingled with energy. I looked up at Thomas once, saw him nod, then began to approach what was left of the well.

Standing over it, my life – up until that exact moment – played before my eyes. The men and women I had tortured or killed, the indecencies I had seen and been a part of in the Dream; all of them surrounded me. I thought about the corruption of the masters, of the soon-to-be unchecked slave trade now that Xzan was not there to control it. Unbidden, Avah Collier came to mind. Avah and her friends discussing the earthquakes and a crack in the sea wall. The quake we had endured in the Wilds was more powerful than I had ever experienced before. Perhaps even now, Atlantis had been swept out to sea, cleansing the land for the living to rebuild. Imagining the grandeur of my city being washed away gave me enough satisfaction to smile. I knew, as the beans fell through my fingers into the infinite hole before me, I wasn't leaving anything I cared about behind.

I hope I get to see the stars.

Chapter 24

Nothing happened. Thomas moved to stand next to me, staring down into the well. "Just wait," he breathed, taking my hand in his. His palm was clammy, and the way he squeezed it hurt my burned fingers; I squeezed back anyway, if only to reassure myself.

Then something did happen.

It was nothing like Thomas had described before. The earth trembled beneath us, though not so much as to knock us to the ground. I looked over at Thomas uncertainly. His eyes were locked on the well with such ferocity I thought he meant to pull the magic from the beans by the sheer force of his will. I could hear the clap of thunder below our feet, and the sound reverberated up the sides of the well until my dream lurched into reality before us.

An enormous geyser of water shot into the sky. The heat from the spray and steam burned our faces, forcing us to back away. The roar was deafening.

"What's going on?" I cried.

Thomas pulled me against his chest, wrapping me in his arms to shield my body from the spray of the water. The earth's tremble became a heaving dance. "I don't know!"

The movement of the ground under our feet grew in its intensity. Just as we were brought to our knees, the world exploded.

Fissures in the ground cracked apart. The well in front of us disappeared in a growing sinkhole that was rapidly taking form. All the while, the geyser increased its ferocity, forcing the earth's maw to open ever wider. I thought Thomas was screaming something at me, but his words were lost in the noise. We scrambled back from Nature's rage, slipping and sliding in mud that had been dust moments only before.

"What do we do?"

I doubted Thomas could hear me any better than I could hear him. His face had taken on a look of serious concentration, his panic carefully contained in the widening whites of his eyes. What he was looking for I didn't know, but I searched around as well. The startling cling of the saturated earth began to pull us down, sucking at limbs like a babe sucks the tit. What we needed was a boat. My eyes fell on the bean plant with its gently folding foliage. The water raining down on us, as warm as it was, had re-invigorated the strange growth of the plant. The leaves were expanding at an alarming rate, at one moment the size of my hand, the next as broad as Thomas' chest.

I hit my fist off Thomas' arm to get his attention, pointing at the leaves where they tugged at the stem as the water and mud tried to pull them away. Thomas understood immediately. We had to wait until a leaf was big enough to climb on to, but that brought with it another problem. The leaf, now the size of a reasonable boat, remained firmly attached to its host by a stem as thick as my thigh. I gave Thomas the knife I had kept from Lark, watching him frantically slice at the only thing holding us down in the muck. While I watched I became aware of a silence descending on us. I looked up.

Everything around me, the chaos of the rippling earth, the steam and debris of the geyser shooting into the heavens, it all went on with as much fury as it had when it first began; however, it was muted somehow. My ears had been stuffed up so I couldn't even hear the frustrated grunts of Thomas at my side every time the blade slipped in his hand.

Then movement on the horizon caught my eye. I had to squint before I could see it well enough to make out the terrible shadow racing toward us. At first it appeared to be a dark band hugging the skyline and growing thicker every second.

When I realized what it was, my heart stopped.

"Thomas!"

He didn't hear me. He was sawing the stem with the small blade with everything he had. Mud was starting to drizzle around our knees though the leaf kept growing as well. He was only halfway through, and the stem continued to thicken.

"Thomas!" I gave his shoulders a good shake. The sound had come back all at once, drowning out the rest of the world once more. My voice was carried away by the din around us. Thomas finally looked up at me long enough to follow the line of my finger pointing back towards Atlantis. His eyes widened before he set back to work with the knife more frantically than before.

I could see it clearly now, the wall of water tumbling towards us. From such a distance, it looked like muddy sap, oozing lazily across the earth; the true nature of its destructive force was becoming clearer with each passing moment too. I could see debris being tossed around. The debris became more distinguishable as it grew closer: a car, a chunk of building, an entire house swept away from the ghetto region of Atlantis. I had never seen the ocean, though I had been atop the wall the Atlantians had used to hold it back. I had heard from those who had seen it, who had stood upon the wall to gaze out at a seemingly endless expanse of water. None of them had ever done justice to the body of death now moving towards us.

With a jerk that sent us toppling into each other, Thomas managed to sever the stem holding our green boat to the bean plant.

The water splashing down from the geyser had already created a dirty pond of water wide enough for six men to lay across. We used our hands to paddle, splashing warm water across our backs in an attempt to go around the geyser before the ocean could bear down on us. As if pulled along an invisible current, our leaf was inevitably drawn towards the pillar of water before us. I looked back over my shoulder at the tidal wave, then over at Thomas. He had stopped paddling.

"Brace yourself!" he screamed loud enough for me to hear. He pulled me towards him, locking one arm around my waist before gripping the side of our flimsy boat with his other hand. I gripped the rough sides of the boat with both hands, hardly feeling the cut of the leaf digging into my skin. Behind us, the wave sent its ominous shadow to block out the suns. Before us, the geyser already tickled the tip of the massive leaf. Closing my eyes, I wondered what it would be like to drown.

Chapter 25

I didn't drown.

The leaf glided into the heart of the geyser as if it were no more than a gentle wave in a pond. That is, until we were fully submerged. Just as I was sure the tidal wave had struck the spot we had occupied a mere heartbeat before, we shot upwards into the sky, carried by boiling water and steam. It felt as though I could see forever in every direction. The force of the pressure beneath us melted away. I looked out over a land completely covered by water in one direction, and slowly being swallowed in the other. Soon, there would be only ocean.

Just as I was wondering how it was that I could breathe in the heart of the waterspout, I realized I couldn't. Thomas had dared to look around as well, but now I saw the struggle in his features as wonder turned into panic. My chest tightened until I had no choice but to open my mouth. The salty water pouring past my lips was drying me out more than a dozen desert suns ever could. The ground beneath us seemed to have disappeared. Only darkness surrounded me. Darkness, and a million shining stars hunting each other across the sky.

Thomas

Thomas held Bella – Xzya – in his arms long after the roar of the water had settled into the subtle muttering of a restless pool. She could have been dead, so cold was her skin against his, but the steady rise and fall of her chest reassured him that life still burned within her.

The air above them was cool. It filled his lungs with the healing powers of a salve, so full of moisture he feared he might drown all over again with each breath. He could feel the sway of their little green boat and finally risked disturbing his companion to sit up and see where they had been deposited. He was sure he was still alive while he held on to the indomitable woman at his side, but letting go of her left him floating helplessly away from reality. Before he could disappear in the encroaching mist, he caught a glimpse of the moon, still whole and unbroken, and knew they had ended up back in his world at last.

"I love you, sweet Belladonna," he whispered with the remaining breath he had in his body.

He was dead now. He was sure of it. The moon and stars had been swallowed by a white mist that hid even his own limbs from sight. Oddly, he could still feel the sway of the boat beneath him, could still hear water lapping at the sides. He strained his eyes against the blinding mist. Was he travelling towards the gates of Heaven or Hell?

Slowly, the mists receded to a hazy fog. Thomas could make out the dark waters surrounding him, see the shallow swells of the current pulling him along. In death, his body felt renewed. He stood, bracing his feet against the motions of the boat, and squared his shoulders against whatever waited for him.

An island loomed ahead of him. Coniferous giants and thick brush hid the interior of the land mass. It couldn't be more than a mile across, with a gently sloping beach of glittering pebbles encircling it like a finely woven girdle around a lady's waist. Their friendly chatter welcomed Thomas as his boat glided into their midst. He felt a sense of peace he had never known before. He marveled at the sensation of stepping out of the boat onto solid ground, the natural roll of cold stones beneath his bare feet felt like a balm next to the hot sand he had traversed. He could smell pine and straw, and the smoke of a hearth carried on a flirtatious breeze. Who knew death would feel so much like coming home?

"Thomas."

Thomas was startled to notice a hooded figure waiting for him near a break in the tree line. He thought it a man, for the figure towered over him in height, as lean as a young oak, yet the voice was decidedly feminine. He started to move forward despite the tingle of trepidation gathering at the base of his skull.

The figure glided over the ground, away from Thomas, leaving no footprints or broken blade of grass to speak to its passing. Thomas followed. Just as he lost sight of the water, they had entered an open area surrounded by a ring of stones.

"What is this?" Thomas demanded. His eyes narrowed when he recognized the formation of rocks a thousand times larger than he. Some had been stood upright, with great slabs stretched across the tops of several pairs. He had seen such a formation before, when Merlin erected one with the other druids of Camelot as their place of mystery. Unlike the Henge in the real world, this one was covered in a myriad of softly glowing ruins. The signs of the druids covered every inch of the stones, like live snakes flowing this way and that. No, not snakes. They looked like the veins of ivory he had marveled at in the beans. A swell of anger served to mask his fear. "Where have you brought me?"

Several more robed figures had stepped into the circle, but the one who had led him there moved to block any retreat he might make. "This place has many names. Some you may have heard before. It is called the Dream by some, Eden by others. You might know this place as Avalon."

Thomas shook his head. "I don't understand. Who are you?"

"We are the Fay, the Dreamers, the Gatekeepers of the Galaxy. We have as many names as we have worlds to watch over."

Thomas looked around him, taking in each hooded figure until he faced the speaker again. It seemed to be the only one interested in answering his questions. "Am I dead?"

The hood tilted, the head within pondering the question. "In your world, in your time, yes. In hers, not yet. She needs you to help her realize her destiny."

Thomas narrowed his eyes. "You speak in riddles."

A heavy sigh disturbed the folds of the hood. "Humans are the simplest of beings. You must always be shown the path before you. Alas, we have no time for explanation. Already darkness is drawing near to her. We will share our knowledge with you as only the Guardians can."

Thomas gasped and retreated when the figure came forward. The hood was pulled back, revealing a long, narrow face and enormous black eyes. The face was almost human in that it also had a small nose and a mouth; the mouth had no lips, and the bulbous head was hairless, with the same white veins as the beans decorating its pale, pink skin. A spider-like hand reached forward, and when it settled on his head, the seven digits outstretched so it could fully encompass Thomas' skull. The little white veins thrummed with power just before a wave of images filled Thomas' head.

In seconds, a thousand worlds came in and out of focus. Thomas saw Camelot, the banners of Arthur waving proudly in the wind. He saw Atlantis, the luminescent towers glittering in defiance of the sea beyond the wall waiting to swallow it. He saw a great wooden ship, its captain brandishing a pistol while wisps of smoke escaped his hat to weave around wild black tendrils of hair. One after the other, some vaguely familiar, some utterly alien, the worlds melted into one another until the magnitude of what he was being shown sucked the breath from Thomas' body. All at once he was weightless, floating in a velvety dark sky full of stars. Each star, too many to count, was a world.

Tears formed at the corners of his eyes. "My god."

"We are one and we are many," a disembodied voice agreed.

"What does this have to do with Bella?"

"She is a Gatekeeper. She has access to each of these worlds and the power to travel between them. She will always attract those who would use her power for ill. Some use it in ignorance, as her previous master did, but others will recognize her true potential. She must learn to harness it, to protect the Gates, before more worlds are destroyed by her ignorance."

The implications of the words settled over Thomas with ominous finality. "You mean Atlantis is gone? Forever?"

"The world of Atlantis was already dying, but yes, the young Gatekeeper ultimately destroyed it. Her anger and regret bent the magic and tore the world apart as you left. Not a great loss, but a dire warning about the breadth of her talents."

Thomas felt his resolve return. He was not dead, and he was not done protecting his lady. "I need to get back to her. How do I help her unlock the rest of her gifts?"

He blinked his eyes, and he was kneeling in the stone circle once more, only the one alien figure remaining. The blinding mists were encroaching on them again. "I will send you back to her now with a map. You must enter the Twelve-Pointed Star and seek out the Gatekeepers there. Once she has been delivered to them, she will be safe, and you will be able to go home."

Thomas might have asked more, but the figure knelt to grasp his left hand. His palm began to sizzle, the pain searing up his arm much the way the electric current of his collar has spread through his body. Just as he would cry out, the pain was gone, and he was kneeling all alone in the mist. On the back of his hand, a scar glowed white against his skin, the strangest kind of map Thomas had ever seen. He had no idea how he would read it, or how he would get to a place he had never heard of in a world that was not his own, but he was going back to Belladonna and that was all that mattered to him.

Chapter 26

When the darkness receded, the first thing I noticed was the soft sound of water tapping against the side of our little craft.

The next thing I noticed was that I was alive.

I sat up sputtering, heaving up any food or water I had consumed in the last week, it seemed. I managed to get most of it over the side, hanging there while I waited for the nausea to pass. Tangled tendrils of my hair trailed against the water's surface, matching its dark beauty. I lifted my eyes to look around. Water was all there was in every direction. Softly churning water, broken only by the leaf on which we sat. *We*! I turned to look frantically for Thomas.

The sight of him where he lay unconscious next to me did little to alter the terror in my heart. The only sign of life in him was the slight rise and fall of his chest. His breathing was too shallow, too slow, but I had no idea how to bring him back to me. Panic rose my gorge until I heaved over the side once more. Tears, or maybe just ocean water trickling out of my hair, chased each other down my cheeks. I had never truly mourned anything as I did then. It was as if I had saved it all for this moment. My mother's death, my grandmother's banishment, the treatment I endured as Xzan's slave. I cried until there was nothing left of me to grieve for. Atlantis was gone. Perhaps lost in some other world. Or maybe it was leagues below me in the very ocean on which I drifted with the man who had given me the courage to take my freedom.

Did he give it to me? I wondered, wiping my eyes to look at him once more. I used a finger to sweep a stray hair from his face. *No, I* thought. He had just shown me what was there all along. My name, the one he had given me, was the armour I had worn to lend me strength. I didn't need it anymore. I was more than Belladonna, beautiful and deadly as the nightshade blossom. I was who I was always meant to be. Xzya, daughter of the most powerful man in Atlantis. Mistress of the Dream.

The sea would not be what killed me.

There was nothing I could do for Thomas. I had no idea how to get into his dreams, if he even had them in the oblivion of unconsciousness, and I had no supplies to make him more comfortable beyond the water bottle I somehow still had on my person. I poured a few trickles through his cracked lips. When it didn't dribble out of the corners of his mouth, I poured a little more before taking a careful sip myself. A small water bottle was little comfort given the uncertainty of the situation.

It was with some wonder I noted only one sun sent its rays to pound on our heads. It was smaller than even our Omega, or so it seemed. I raised a hand to shield my eyes while I marveled at the bright white orb in an infinite cerulean sky. Soft white clouds floated here and there, swirling lazily on a breeze that didn't deem it necessary to make its way down to tousle my hair. My wonder didn't last with the realization one sun could be nearly as hot as two. It reflected mercilessly off the water in a double assault.

Night came.

At first, the rapidly setting sun filled me with renewed terror. How would I survive weeks of darkness in a world I had no way to navigate? The further the sun sank, the more I dreaded the ominous waters. I swore I could see creatures circling in its depths. I thought myself crazy, until one of the creatures broke the surface, a jagged point of shiny rubber that cut the water like a knife before sinking once more. No, not rubber. Whatever the creature was – Thomas had never shown me creatures of the sea during our Dreams – it soon had companions. I could feel them nudge the bottom of our little boat greedily in the night. All I could do was pray our boat, a boat which was really no more than the flimsy green foliage of a beanstalk, could withstand the curious jostling from below. Terror made me lay myself alongside Thomas' prone body, absorbing his warmth and imagining him as my shield.

I wondered if he knew what the water creatures were and had chosen not to show me.

Terror began to abate. I may have slept for a time. I closed my eyes to control the fear only to open them to the full darkness of night. The full moon in the sky was brilliantly whole, a complete, radiant orb shining out over the world as if to console its inhabitants and banish the nightmares. Millions upon millions of stars stood out next to it, little sentinels lending the strength of their light to the moon. I wept again, and through the blurry vision of my tears I thought I saw them: the legends from my grandmother's stories. My eyes traced the lines of stars where they clustered in an orderly fashion, and I told and retold myself the story of the Warrior and his Huntress, of the Twins and their dire warning, and of every other being I had ever heard of but never seen. I fell asleep trying to count them all. Before my eyes could fully close, I saw one star fall and remembered something my grandmother had said once. *One may wish upon a falling star.* The Warrior had wished for his perfect mate. I wished for salvation.

Night and day interchanged much more quickly in this new world. Because of this, I knew it was the third day when my carefully rationed water ran out. Still, Thomas had not woken up. Twice he had spoken in his sleep, muttering strange names or cursing magic beans. Once he threw such a fit, I thought we would both be cast into the waters with the monsters lurking there, yet I managed to settle him down again with no more than my soothing voice and my hands moving gently up and down his arms. At night, I tried to enter his dreams, but his mind was no more than a storm cloud. Each time I tried to enter, lightning would strike out at me, sending me back to myself. I hated to think he was trapped in there, yet I found some comfort knowing his soul still fought so valiantly. I could only hope it returned to his body before the physical Thomas wasted away.

Once the water was gone there was nothing left to do but lay next to Thomas and die along with him. I watched the lonely sun make its solitary journey across the sky. I reveled in the soothing moonlight while images of animals and warriors took shape in the stars. And every now and then, one of the stars would shoot across the sky and I would wish for the same things:

I wished for rescue.

I wished for Thomas to wake up.

On the fourth day, my wishes came true.

Chapter 27

There were more clouds in the sky on the fourth morning. They were an ominous grey, more like smoke than the soft pillows I had grown accustomed to. When our boat struck a solid surface, startling me out of a deep sleep, they were the first thing I noticed. Disoriented by this small change, I rolled over to see Thomas' eyes were open and staring. My heart leapt to my throat.

"Thomas, you're awake!" I cried, taking his face in both my hands. I moved to kiss his face, his lips, a blister on his nose, laughing even as my tears of relief fell upon his cheeks. I stopped when I realized he was blinking in total astonishment, his eyes staring at something beyond me. Following his gaze, I raised my eyes to the thing we had hit.

The side of it curved well over our heads, the dark patterns of its surface tugging at the eye until I was too distracted to notice the small openings where the dull glint of iron caught the sun. I reached out a hand to touch its rough surface, sliding fingers along the material made slick by the ocean. When I pulled them to rub together in front of my eyes, an odd resin made my fingers greasy. Thomas was trying to sit up next to me, but weakness from the days he had spent asleep sent him back down.

"Oi!"

The voice was so unexpected neither of us knew where to look. Thomas was the first to look skyward again. When I followed suit, I finally noticed the row of surly faces staring down at us. "Thomas?" My voice was a cracked whisper even in my own ears.

Thomas didn't respond.

A man, with a rather toothless grin, rested his weight on one casual elbow as he spoke. "Now how 'n the 'ell did the likes of ye two find yerselfs scuffing up the side of ol' *Revenge?* After I just scrubbed 'er down, too."

It sounded to me as if he had chewed up his words before spitting them down on us, but the light in Thomas' eyes sparkled with new life.

"Are you an Englishman?" He called out, voice hoarse after days without water.

The round of laughter from the men above told us Thomas had been heard. "Oh, aye," the one said, revealing how little teeth he really had to chew his words with. "I be an Englishman. Question is, what kinna Englishman are you?"

Thomas glanced at me, a troubled expression muting the hope I had seen there only moments before. "I don't understand your question," he admitted at last.

Laughter rippled among the onlookers. The first speaker leaned heavily on muscled arms. I swore I could feel his spittle on my face, and it was as salty as the sea. "I mean, do ye serve the king or do ye serve yerself?"

Thomas' mouth snapped shut. I couldn't grasp the meaning of this exchange, unable to imagine what a king was outside of what little Thomas had taught me. If a king must be served, then he was no better than a Master. Just as Thomas seemed to settle on what to say, I raised my voice over his.

"We serve ourselves," I declared, rising in our wobbling boat in the best display of defiance I could manage.

The men overhead examined us both in silence for seconds that seemed to drag on for eternity. My entire body felt ready to dive into the water, ready to drown before being taken by these strangers. Thomas' thigh against mine was just as tense. At last, the laughter burst forth again and on some invisible signal a rope was tossed down to us.

"Well, that be good," the toothless man grinned at us. "From what we hear, the new king is a real twat. Cap'n Thatch'll have the final say, but ye might as well come up for a spell before we toss ye back to the sea."

As it turned out, neither one of us had the strength to climb the rope. Even Thomas could scarcely sit-up before a wave of dizziness cast him back down. I tied the rope around his waist, helping him to stand so the men in the vessel could pull him up. At first, he protested, insisting that I go first.

"And you think they will throw the rope back down for a half-drowned man like you," I whispered to him with as little insult as I could. "I have been in the minds of men, remember? If they mean me harm, they will not hesitate to let you drift away if only to save the strength it would take to raise you up for the fun they can have with me."

I saw by the wince in Thomas' brow that he still disliked the story of my past, but he could not offer any logic against mine to sway me. Indeed, his voice seemed to have abandoned him altogether. His eyes were bursting with secrets I knew he wanted to share, but it would have to wait until our safety was secured. I watched him rise unsteadily over my head. Something in the back of my mind wondered where his unconscious mind had gone. I was determined to ask him as soon as the opportunity arose. As it was, after Thomas had disappeared over the side of the ship, I wondered if perhaps men in this world had other tastes. It was agonizing to wait for my turn at rescue.

In the end, the rope was cast back down for me to tie around my own waist. The lurching movement of their efforts took the wind from my chest. The strange green leaf, our life-saving vessel when the tides of magic had carried us away, sank below the surface of the sea as soon as my feet left as if it had never been meant to float there at all.

Rough hands pulled me onto the deck of the much larger boat we had encountered; they didn't release me even once I found my feet beneath me to stand. For a moment I was grateful, while I waited for dizziness to pass, but then the iron in their grip became shackles from which I could not break away. A cup of stale water was held to my lips. I drank gratefully once I saw Thomas do the same, but I watched the men around me the way I would watch any of Xzan's proposed targets. Studying them could prove to be my only hope of surviving them.

The first thing I noticed was their skin. While several of the men had sun-drenched skin as pale as Thomas if removed from the light, several of them were like the night come alive. Their eyes seemed to glow against their ochre skin; teeth, where they still remained in pink gums, seemed whiter than they actually were if only by comparison. I soon realized we must be in a land closer to Thomas' than mine, if only by the size of the humans all around me. Two of the largest black men held Thomas between them like he was hardly more than a child. Of the rest, none were much shorter I was sure, and all of them boasted surly muscles and swagger enough for a hundred men of Atlantis. They wore all manner of garments; every one of them was different from my own. Ragged vests stretched out over broad chests on some, while billowing white shirts clung to the sweat-soaked backs of others. Most of the men wore no shoes and their baggy pants, cut short at the ankle, were held at their waists by all manner of belts and sashes.

It seemed none of them spoke the same tongue either, their dialects and languages as different as the clothes on their backs. Thomas' tongue was easy enough to pick up, but the clipped barks of some of the darker men and the lilting song of the some of the paler ones, became a melody that left me feeling lost and more than a little stunned. It was only when silence fell over them all, I began to find the ability to concentrate on what was going to happen to us.

Our fate stepped forward in shiny black boots that clicked against the deck like the echo of a tap left to drip into the sink.

The boots belonged to a man taller than Thomas, a man whose slender frame moved with the fluid grace of a dancer. The boat swayed with the gentle rhythm of the sea and this man swayed with it. A black beard hid half of his face, and equally dark hair sprouted with unruly curls from beneath a broad hat. Though the sun, as lonely as it was, cast its heavy warmth over us, the fearsome man before us wore a great overcoat with his pants tucked into the tops of his boots. Between his hairy visage, and the excessive finery he wore, the only features I could see were the piercing blue of his eyes and the straight line of his nose.

If there were masters in this world, there was no doubt in my mind I was face-to-face with the lord of them all. He appraised me with such ruthless disdain I could not help but lower my eyes back to the toes of his boots. It was as much a survival instinct as a display of submission.

"I thought ye said ye served only yerself, lass. Don't be bowing now on account of me."

I looked up through the tangle of my lashes, surprised by the cold humour in his eyes. His appraisal had changed from one of appreciation to one of disappointment. A dark eyebrow was raised in question.

"I only meant to show my respect," I replied softly, affecting my most sultry voice. It was difficult to do when my clothes hung in tattered disrepair and my hair was wilder than his. "I am unfamiliar with the practices of your land."

The man smirked while the rest of the crew suppressed muffled laughter.

"Fine talker," he scoffed, stepping closer to me. The smell of his sweat clogged my nose, which scarcely came to his chest. "Foreigner for certain, and a lady, too, I reckon. Where are ye from, lass?"

I tried desperately not to glance at Thomas, uncertain how to respond. "Doesn't matter where I'm from," I told him, trying not to let my voice betray the way my knees wobbled beneath me. "I'm not going back there."

Those eyes could have pierced my very soul, I was sure of it. His stare crashed into me with the force of the ocean, the window to his Dream obscured by the tempest there. In my search for a way in, I missed whatever conclusions the man drew about me. For several minutes, I was struggling to breathe. Then the air around me cleared and I could allow myself to slouch between my captors when the man's attention was turned to Thomas. I was a little apprehensive about Thomas' response to his authority; he had scarcely demonstrated humility in the past; this man made Xzan seem like a petulant child.

"He's an Englishman, cap'n," Toothless grinned. "Sounds like a Welshman if ye ask me."

Thomas spit what little he could. "No one's asking you."

Toothless' amicable nature changed in an instant. His fist cracked against the side of Thomas' face. A moment later he smiled once more. "Meant no offence, lad. We've plenty o' Welshmen on board here."

The captain was unimpressed by the display. "Not Welsh, then." He seemed to be smiling. "I was a Norfolk man myself. Can't say it's something I brag about, either. Like to think I'm a man of the world now."

Thomas didn't seem to know what to say. He was in no state to fight his way free, though I saw the thought of it pass through his eyes. Besides, even he must recognize that there was nowhere to go. Our little boat had sunk and there was nothing but ocean around us. The silence on the ship seemed to be waiting on something, some interaction yet to take place.

Thatch broke the silence first. "What's an Englishman doing with a foreign lady, lost at sea and with scarcely a scrap of clothing between the two of ye. Did ye steal her away from her father, lad, but forgot how to steer the ship?"

Laughter echoed around us.

Thomas remained stoic. Perhaps he didn't know what to say. Perhaps he was choosing to remain silent. My own frayed nerves were running out of patience and my stomach reminded me how long it had been since we'd had something to eat. Thatch turned to me. "Isn't much of a talker, is he?"

I glanced at Thomas long enough for me to see the shake of his head. Turning to Thatch I tried to speak as though to an equal. "We have been at sea so long I can't be sure if it has been only weeks or a whole month. Our food ran out days ago, our water shortly after that. If we had not bumped into your vessel, we would have sunk along with the little boat your men pulled us from." I paused to shoot a warning glance at Thomas. "Forgive Thomas, his weakness makes him surly."

Thatch glanced back at Thomas, too. "Seems like a strong enough lad with a bit of food and water to bolster him. I'm not one to waste such luxuries on a man who can't work for it though. Bones, go ahead and toss that one back to the sea. Mayhap Davey Jones will smile on us for slaking his hunger with such a fine whelp."

Thomas found the strength to fight then. He jerked and leapt between his captors, but the grip of the men could not be broken. The sound of a growl rose from his throat while a desperate cry escaped from my own lips when they got close enough to lift him over the railing. "Please stop!" I wrenched myself free from the men holding me; they likely hadn't expected me to fight them. I pulled my knife from my boot and drew blood from the first man who attempted to regain a hold on me. "Leave him!"

Everything froze again when the captain raised a hand. It sparkled with wide gold bands on three of his fingers. Thomas was still being held, hung over the side of the ship by his ankles. In the silence, I realized Thatch was waiting on me.

My eyes met his and I searched for the window there. "I'll," I swallowed, my knife slipping in my sweaty palms. "I'll show you great pleasure if you spare him."

The laughter from the onlookers startled me. The look in the captain's eyes turned my bowels to water. "Oh lass, ye'll be laying with me anyway. By the time we reach Tortuga, ye'll be familiar with a good deal of my mates, too, I imagine."

I swallowed the horror threatening to overwhelm me. I stood straighter, tossing my hair with every ounce of Xzan's self-assured grace I could manage. I was walking on the edge of something bigger than me, I could feel it. While I wasn't sure what line I trudged, I was sure one misstep would be worse than a slip on Xzan's pedestals.

"Mr. Thatch, if you spare my companion, I will show you such pleasure you'll cut the cock off the next man who even tries to take me to his bed."

The chuckling stopped then as each man watched their captain for his response. Thatch stepped right into the tip of my short blade. I raised my chin in response; I had to bite the inside of my cheek to keep my lip from trembling. "Ye got the royal treasury between yer legs, do ye, lass?"

"Some days, if I'm in the mood," I said, my voice lowered for him alone. "Sometimes it's a swift death for the man who takes me when I'm not willing," I finished, my voice lowering further until it was hardly more than a whisper.

"Ye think ye can kill me with a little thing like this?" His hand closed over mine on the hilt of my knife with surprising speed.

"It worked well enough on my brother."

An ember of desire came to life in his eyes then, and with it, the window I was looking for cracked open. It was too small to penetrate, but for the first time I was certain I could wedge it wide enough to take him to the Dream. If my energy held up anyway.

"Bones," Thatch barked, his breath hot against my face. "Take the codfish downstairs and hang him up to dry. Give him just enough food and water to keep him alive until morning."

I raised an eyebrow. "Only morning?"

"I'll be needin' to see the royal treasure for myself before I decided whether or not yer man dies."

Thatch pulled me into his side, one arm resting casually enough around my shoulder to rest a hand comfortably on one breast. When Thomas was pulled right side up, his ferociousness was renewed at the sight of it.

"No, Bella! Don't! You don't have to do this."

I cringed when I heard the hurt anger in his voice, even after he had disappeared somewhere below deck. He wasted precious energy on such fighting. I had none to waste on pity.

"Open the sails, boys," Thatch shouted to his men. "We've booty to deliver and women to fuck." He gave me a good shake. "I think I'll start with this one!"

A roar of approval followed us as I was swung over the captain's shoulders and carried below deck. Mold and the smell of the sea was enough to make me faint. Somehow, I clung to my wits until I was set down, rather roughly, on a closed, round barrel.

I looked around at the other barrels surrounding us, at the crates and casks and other rubbish. When I looked back at the man before me, he had shed his coat and was offering me a silver flask. "Where is the bed?"

Thatch laughed. "No bed, lass. If I like ye the lads won't begrudge me one of the cabins tonight, but I'm not one for such comforts. They make a man soft."

Thirst made me take a gulp from the flask, only to be laughed at once more when my body shook with a fit of coughing. "This isn't water."

"Rum, lass," Thatch said in a low rumble, his hands already trying to find the warm spot near the top of my thighs. "Never met a woman who didn't like a drink before a romp."

"You've never met a woman like me," I assured him when I could find my breath. His body wedged itself between my thighs, his hands traveling up towards my breasts. His beard tickled where he nuzzled my neck.

Maybe it was the rum filling my empty stomach, or maybe it was the startling way his hands alternated between gentle massage and demanding squeeze, but my light-headedness made me lean into his caress the way a cat leans into its master's hand. It was only my own purr of delight that brought me back to the task at hand. I pulled his head back, bracing myself to stare into the terrifying tempest of his eyes. The window was still there, so I reached a hand down to where his body fought the confines of his trousers. There was little to get in the way of my hand and I soon found a smooth rhythm I could maintain in my weakened state.

He groaned and tried to lean in to nibble at my neck once more, but I stopped him. He was surprised but aroused by the challenge in my eyes. I held him that way, feeding his arousal with my defiance while I watched his walls come down. "How is it so far?" I asked, my breath as ragged as his.

"Still waiting on that treasure, lass," he pulled my body tighter against him, but he didn't break eye contact.

"A little patience," I grinned, watching as my window became an open door. Leaning in, I whispered in his ear. "Where do you want me?"

Thomas

The floorboards groaned when Thomas shoved his shoulder against them with every ounce of strength he could find. This wasn't going to happen again, not again. Thatch would not take her from him. His teeth ached from the force of his jaw clenching against a cry of frustration.

A boot stomped above his head. "Knock it off or it ain't gonna matter how much the cap'n likes your lass. I'll be tossing ye overboard meself."

Thomas scowled at the shadow moving above his head, but he refrained from fighting against the door again. Instead, he let himself step down the short ladder to the floor of the ship's hold. He couldn't risk being tossed from the ship. He would have to wait, to bide his time until someone was foolish enough to open the hatch and let him out. With a little rest he would be ready to fight, and he would make sure Thatch was sorry for any harm he caused.

Before allowing the big men to release him, Bones had left a flask and a smelly sack on a barrel near the back of the hold. Thomas decided to try his luck with whatever fortune he had left. The flask was full of tepid water. After a few tentative sips, Thomas emptied the contents of the sack. A few strips of dried fish, a wrinkled apple, and a hard chunk of cheese made up a feast fit for a prisoner. After years of nothing more than the ENSA cubes in Atlantis, Thomas struggled to chew the tough, leathery fish. He decided to eat the cheese and fruit first. When he was sure his stomach would not reject what had once been an average meal for him, he sucked on a strip of fish and searched his surroundings for a weapon.

There was nothing around him save barrel upon barrel of strange spices and wooden crates filled with all manner of silks and fine linens. Small circular openings in the wall let in the sunlight by which he could see the hopelessness of his search. Thomas knew this was no trading vessel. The men were too hardy, and too quick to murder. While he couldn't fathom what kind of bandits they could be, he began to feel the effects of his time asleep. The hooded figure from his dreams came to mind, and he rushed to one of the portholes to examine the back of his hand under the light.

The figure had said it was a map, but it made no sense to Thomas at all. The image began with a triangle. In the center of the triangle was an eye, its life-like detail giving him the sense that it watched him though it appeared to be no more than white ink etched into his skin. From the top and bottom, and from either side of the eye, straight lines stretched out beyond the boundaries of the triangle. Thomas counted the points of the triangle and the end of each line. Seven. The Seven-Pointed Star. Other symbols he did not recognize had been etched at each point as well. They looked like letters, but not any letter he had ever encountered. Then again, he had only learned to read after reaching Atlantis, and their script was much different that he remembered from his own land.

He just needed to find someone to read the script.

The rustle of bare feet above his head caught his attention again. First, he would need to find someone he could trust enough to share this secret with. Until then...Thomas took a length of linen from one of the crates and ripped off a strip of it. He tied it around his hand until his new scar was effectively hidden from view.

He drank some more water before he settled down to wait. They would come for him soon and he'd be ready.

End of Book 1

Preview of Book 2:
Stars in the Devil's Eye

Edward

Edward sidled up to his mother, pressing his grubby face into the soft folds of her skirt. One small finger became hooked in a hole in the linen she hadn't found the time to repair. The frayed threads tangled around the slender digit, cutting into tender flesh as surely as the noose cut into the neck of the prisoner before them.

Edward didn't understand the scene playing out before him. The way the man jerked at the end of the rope made Edward's knees tremble as though they meant to join in the odd dance. Something warmed the inside of his pant legs. Why was this happening? He wanted to go home, not watch the strangled squeals of a man struggling too fiercely to cling to a life he'd already lost.

Edward tried to bury his face in his mother's skirt, but she stopped him. "Ye look, Edward. Look and remember the price of foolish pride."

Edward looked up at the woman next to him instead. Margaret Thatch's black curls were as wild and frenzied as her dark eyes. Thin white lines had carved trails on her cheeks where earlier tears had cut their way through the grime on her face. There was no more time for grief than there was for torn skirts.

Finally, the man died.

The crowds dispersed.

These executions were becoming commonplace. It was a relief when they mixed it up a bit with a burning or a beheading. James was the king in England now. The execution of over three hundred rebels had more than settled the matter. Better a Catholic on the throne than a bastard, same said.

Others just kept their damn mouths shut.

The ghosts of the remaining few rebels dangled next to the latest hangman's toy.

Edward held fast to his mother's hand lest they be torn apart by the smothering crowd now trying to clear the square. Shit and piss stained the hem of his mother's skirts, but Edward deftly avoided the putrid puddles and suspicious mounds of mud as they allowed the flow of people to guide them away from the macabre display of tyranny.

When they reached their little brick house in East London, Margaret paused only long enough to tear the eviction notice from their door before shutting them safely inside. For several long minutes, Margaret leaned heavily against the door while Edward shifted uncomfortably in his soiled breeches. They'd grown cold and the rough fabric chafed his skin. At last, she let out a heavy sigh and slid down to open her arms wide for her son.

Edward didn't hesitate to throw himself at her. She ignored the stench of urine on his clothes, and he wanted to drown in the scent of her perfume. She held him that way for a moment of eternity before standing and straightening out her clothes.

"Let's have some supper," Margaret took an apron from a peg. "Our last supper before yer granddad comes for us tomorrow."

Though he knew the answer, Edward asked the question forever on a four-year-old's lips: "Why?"

"Because Mr. Baxter can't take care of us anymore and I need to find a job." Pots clattered together while she searched for the right one.

"Why?"

"Because without a job we'll be out on the streets," she paused in her efforts to light their little stove. "I won't lettum take ye away. Now, be a good lad and go change out of those dirty trousers."

The very thought of being taken away made Edward tremble. He couldn't know it was what kept his mother up most nights as well. She had fought her parents when the man she loved had left her unwed and alone. She had fought the late Mr. Baxter who hated children but was willing to pay their rent to have a good wench at home, cooking and cleaning and warming his bed. She had never been one to give up without fighting for what she needed to survive.

The iron will of a survivor had served her well most of her life.

Now, Mr. Baxter was dead. A victim of an oversized mouth. He hadn't even been a true rebel, just a boisterous drunk who liked to spin tall tales in the pub. Margaret had had no choice but to write her father for help. The alternative was to risk sending Edward to the orphanage and losing him forever. She had heard many women lament the loss of a child in such a way; left in the hands of God's servants while they searched for work, then never seen again after the Church adopted them out to be labourers in the country. No one would take her son from her.

The sun went down. There were no lamps lit on their little street, so they were swallowed by a darkness held at bay by the waning glow of the candles on their table. It didn't bother either of them.

When the old pottage had been scraped from the pot to fill their stomachs, mother and son played a game of dice so Edward could practice his numbers. He was getting much better at counting past the number of fingers he had. He was just starting to yawn when Margaret handed him the wooden cup for one last roll.

Three dice clattered to the floor just as thunder crashed through the door and lightning illuminated the devil himself.

Edward stared at the two dice still left on the table. Snake eyes. He shivered in his seat.

"What're ye doing here?" Margaret demanded of the men entering her kitchen. She stood between the interlopers and her precious son. "The law says I have 'till tomorrow to leave."

A harsh chuckle. "Oh, dearie, are ye forgetting the size o' yer debt, then? The law cares little for those who can't pay their debts."

"What?" Margaret's body tensed.

"Baxter owed me two months' rent," the man said, casually taking a seat at their table. Weak candlelight cast ominous shadows over his face, filling deep pock-marks with shadows and giving already sallow skin a sickly glow. "Tis a shame the poor sap's dead but I got to thinkin', ye bein' 'is woman and all, ye'd be settling his debt before ye disappeared on me."

Margaret swallowed. "I can't pay the debt. I've nothing to pay it with. My father'll be here tomorrow, though. I'm sure he'd be happy to pay."

Edward cowered behind his mother. He couldn't follow the flow of conversation, but his eyes never left the two other shadows that shifted impatiently near the doorway.

"I'm a busy man, Ms. Thatch. Headed to Cornwall tomorrow for a spell. I'm afraid I'll be needin' the money now."

The shadows from the doorway broke away from their posts. Edward whimpered softly as he watched them circle around to stand behind his own chair. He might have scurried under the table, but coal-blackened hands pressed him deeper into his seat.

Margaret noticed the other men too late to pull Edward from their grip. Dark eyes narrowed on the tears she fought to keep in check. "I can't pay ye what I don't have," she spoke through clenched teeth.

The man stood from the table and sauntered towards Margaret on a lanky frame. "I'm sure ye can think o' something that'll satisfy, Ms. Thatch."

What little gap remained between them was closed when he grabbed the young woman by the arm and pulled her into him. She grimaced when he buried his face into her neck, pressing her hands against his chest in a vain attempt to push him away. Her eyes found Edward's and disgust was sharpened by her own maternal fear.

"Not in here."

The man's face turned towards Edward. The little boy stuck out his chin bravely, though the broken yellow teeth sneering at him gave birth to demons in his soul.

"The boy's gotta learn some time," he chuckled before resuming his lecherous demands. Edward watched his mother watching him. He didn't realize he was her perfect mirror image: black eyes, black curling hair, and the subtle shift in the set of their jaw from fright to fight.

Margaret smiled at her son. "Always fight, little luv. Yer never truly beat 'till yer dead in the ground."

The man had pulled back his head when she started to speak. There was a flash of movement as Margaret snapped her head forward, and his nose was suddenly bleeding profusely from an odd angle against his face. Margaret was able to break free of his grasp and turn away.

"Bitch!" he gurgled. He lunged at Margaret, twisting her back around before landing his right fist against the side of her face. Bones cracked.

Edward screamed when his mother's body hit the ground. The shadow hands gripping his shoulders struggled to hold down his own bucking body. "Momma!"

The stranger dove at Margaret's prone form. Edward broke free at last and charged into the man's side. His screams and his pummeling fists were rewarded with a heavy backhand that sent him sprawling.

Shadows danced in and out of focus after that. Edward thought he saw his mother renew her vigorous defiance of her attacker. He thought he saw the devil wrap his hands around her throat and suck out her soul.

He thought he saw her rise from her body and float away from him, surrounded by an ethereal white light.

"Wake up, lad."

The voice in his ear was gruff, frightening in its strangeness, but Edward obeyed the command. He looked up into blue, red-rimmed eyes set deeply in a craggy old face. The man scooped Edward up into his arms. "Let's go, Edward."

"Are you my granddad?"

"Yes."

"Where's Momma?"

The old man grunted and sniffed once before he replied. "She's gone home to God, lad."

"Why?"

Edward began to squirm in his grandfather's arms. "Settle down, boy."

"Momma!"

Edward caught a glimpse of morning light on pale skin on the floor before he was carried from the only home he had ever known. His heart turned to ice when recognition settled on him. It was Margaret, her face a mass of purple mincemeat. One eye bulged out of its socket. A tooth rested on the floor like discarded treasure.

It was Margaret, but it was no longer his mother.

While his grandfather carried him away from the broken body to sit him on the bench of an old cart, Edward felt a storm rising in his soul that swept away the memories of the woman he used to love.

****

The fabric of the Dream trembled.

My vision blurred and the reality of a quaint, little kitchen with its ghastly scene began to evaporate in a red haze. All I could sense was a bottomless pit of rage, and it wasn't coming from me. I was still too weak from being lost at sea, which barely allowed me the energy to feel mildly surprised by what I had just witnessed. My control of the Dream teetered perilously close to the edge of its limits. In less than a moment, I was cast back into my body like a boulder crashing into a puddle. The sensation made me sick. The voice bellowing in my head made me vomit.

"Stay out!"

The real world was as unfocused as the Dream. I was still sitting on a wooden barrel, the stench of sea water and sweat blending with the new mess down the front of my shirt. I fell forward against the chest of the strange man before me, gasping for breath. Visions of the past several days swirled through my mind: the days I had spent wandering a desert, searching for an escape from a world where the corruption of Atlantis was given a place to exist; the terror of finding myself lost at sea. It was a mess of seemingly contradicting scenarios, yet oddly no less normal than being thrust, uninvited, into a stranger's memories. Memories, I got the distinct impression, that were not for me to see.

Edward Thatch, dark eyes glittering from beneath the brim of his hat, yanked back my head with a fistful of my hair. He didn't seem to notice the slime of bile against my chin. "Ye mind tellin' me what that was about?"

"I-I'm not sure," I hedged. Really, I wasn't sure at all, but my fear left me bereft of even a false explanation.

Those eyes were infinitely deadlier than the lustful rage I had grown used to in my half-brother, Lark. He hadn't known he was my brother when he had used the Dream to torture me, forcing my body to service every deprived fantasy he could come up with. Lark had seen who I truly was, what I could do, and he had recognized the power it could give him. Fortunately, I began to realize my own power too. Realization left only one of us alive. I knew without meeting the black pools of his eyes, that I would not be so lucky with the man in front of me.

Thatch decided to believe me. Or so I thought. One moment I was staring into the face of death – wondering how I came to be in such a ridiculous situation – and the next, I was being dragged further down a corridor to a ladder leading deep into the gullet of the ship. The bone-crushing grip previously being used on my forearm disappeared the same moment I noticed the floor disappear beneath me. It was a short fall to the wooden boards below, but the impact took the wind from me none-the-less.